GOT OUT
THE GAME

GOT OUT
THE GAME

by
DAULA DAY

A TRUE STORY TOLD THROUGH A MOTHER'S EYES

GOT OUT THE GAME

Printing History

First Printing: December, 2011

In this book, the names of individuals have been changed for their
privacy.

For further information visit dkeveryday.com

ISBN 978-0-615-55386-3

Dedicated to all of the single mothers
who are raising fatherless sons.

CONTENTS

PREFACE

I was born in Baton Rouge, Louisiana. My parents had seven children: three boys and four girls, of whom I am the second-oldest daughter and third-oldest child. We were all raised by our biological parents. Everyone in our family called our father, who was a World War II veteran, "Daddy." He was very strict, smart, hard-working, and a good provider. He was known to be very frank and would tell anyone exactly what was on his mind. Our father was not a tall man; he was approximately five feet eight inches tall.

I remember getting whipped with an extension cord for not coming straight home from school to do my chores. My father was not shy when it came to administering whippings. His grandmother had been a slave in Georgia, and had given my father his share of beatings whenever he got out of line. Our father did not tolerate children misbehaving and disobeying their parents.

Our mother, whom everyone called "Mama," was the opposite of Daddy. She was a beautiful lady who stood about five feet eleven inches tall. She had very high cheekbones that had been inherited from her grandmother, who was a Native American. Mama was wise, kind, and did not whip any of her children. However, she never disputed any of our father's decisions when it came to disciplining us.

Childhood greatly influences what we become as adults. That is why I chose education as my major in college. I have been teaching the second grade for the past thirty years, and I am currently an instructor for new teachers. I advise them on how to administer their daily teaching activities, and on how to prepare their lesson plans. Regrettably, like many teenage girls, I fell in love with a "bad boy" from my neighborhood of Rockwood. I thought it would be fun and exciting to date a tough guy. I did not want to be with a cowardly man who was afraid to protect himself or me. Well, I was impregnated by this "bad boy" three times. After the third child, I finally realized that it was time to end my relationship with him. It was obvious that he was not going to change his thuggish ways, and therefore, I did not see a future with him. I would spend the remaining years of my young life raising my children alone.

After I had my kids, my father gave me the lecture of my life. He said, "Daula, you are going to take care of your babies and finish college."

Daddy also insisted that I not get a job, and he paid my way through college. I was grateful and very fortunate for that. Unlike many people, I did not have to take out student loans and graduate in debt.

Raising children as a single mother is a difficult task, and raising boys is even more of a challenge. They really need a male figure in the household to be their role model. I had my first child, Renae, when I was sixteen, and my second child, Willie, when I was seventeen. My other two children, Monique and Gerrod, were born within the next seven years, though Gerrod had a different father than my first three kids.

Even though I had children at an early age, I did not use that as an excuse to give up my goals. I attended college and obtained a degree in education. I was determined! And I instilled that drive in my children. I also made sure that my sons and daughters did not have children at an early age. I did not allow my daughters to date until they were eighteen years old; I put both of them on birth control pills, and gave condoms to my sons. Renae took the pill with no problem, but Monique did not. I would have to call Monique into my bedroom and watch her take the pill. Thankfully, she did not get pregnant until she got married and had a son, Lil' Tanky, whom everyone thinks favors his Uncle Willie. Maybe Monique's son favors her brother since she always gave him such a hard time growing up. She sure got a kick out of harassing her big brother! We had only one television in the house, and those two fought constantly over it. Willie and Monique never wanted to watch the same thing, so I made a rule that gave the person who turned the television on first the right to watch whatever he or she wanted that day. Of course, Monique would wake up early on Saturday mornings just to stop her brother from watching his college football games. She would sit there and not even watch the television, and that drove him crazy! She would also get under his skin with her food: Monique would not eat her cheeseburgers from McDonald's, and whenever her brother would ask for it, she would tell him no. Willie would sneak a bite out of it after realizing that his little sister was just trying to piss him off again, and Monique would come running into my room, crying that Willie was eating her food. This back-and-forth went on with them all time. Those two damn kids got on my last nerve.

I remember telling one guy who came to our house to date my oldest daughter, Renae, "Young man, Renae is only sixteen years old and she is not allowed to have company."

The young gentleman politely said, "Yes, ma'am," and walked away.

Ironically, he was the guy whom Renae would eventually marry at eighteen, and they are still married to this day. They also have two wonderful children, Boogie and Jazz.

The book you are about to read includes things that happened in my oldest son's life. Some incidents negatively influenced his younger brother, cousins, and other youngsters in the neighborhood to follow in his footsteps. We see this pattern in most of the inner cities across the United States. I am writing this book because my son could easily have been another statistic, but got a second chance and made good of it. Young men of color overpopulate our prisons, where their brilliant minds are not put to use. There are potential doctors, lawyers, scientists, writers, entrepreneurs, and engineers locked away in our prison systems at this very moment. This cycle of our young men going to prisons has been occurring for many decades.

However, there are no definite strategies, methods, or solutions to help alleviate these problems. I'm not saying that I have all the answers, but I would like to offer my opinion on some things that I thought could be helpful. Some things that I was able to experience while raising my son, and would like to share, are the following:

A growing boy should mow the lawn under supervision, and perform yard or garden work. In my opinion, it helps him become a responsible man.

A child must complete his homework before watching television, playing video games, or being allowed to do any other extracurricular activities.

He should not talk back to his parents. This tends to lead to him disrespecting people in authority.

This behavior contributes to your child becoming dependent on you for everything in life, and furthermore, becoming an irresponsible man. This follows the same principle as teaching someone to fish so that they can learn to feed themselves: do not baby or spoil your son.

He should take out the trash.

He should keep the vehicles clean, inside and out.

Disciplining him is a must!

Do not pay him for work done around the house; however, praise him for a job well done.

The ages of thirteen to fourteen are the transitional years: your son is struggling with who, what, and where he wants to be in life at this stage. You could lose him forever during this period. This is a very critical time!

Be very mindful of peer pressure during this period.

Even if all of the things previously mentioned are done, your son's environment, friends, family, and personal decisions are often the most important factors in determining his future. They were in my case. I disciplined my son and did not baby him. However, his decisions, friends, and environment got the best of him.

However, any of my experiences you choose to share with your son will help him make good, sound choices in life.

Some incidents in this book are very dramatic and helped shape my son Willie into the person he is today. He and I had plenty of discussions together while writing this book. It is really amazing to me, the type of memory he possesses. He can remember things from as far back as when he was a toddler. He shocked me when he described the time he got out of his bed one night and crawled into the living room, where his father and I had been talking. He told me that I'd come over to him and picked him up from the floor, and that I then placed him between his father and me, and gave him some saltine crackers to eat because he had been crying.

He described it quite well, down to the part where he had been afraid to get out of the bed in case he fell to the floor. He told me that the floor had appeared to be so far away. My son had sat up in the bed and, when he did not see me, crawled to the edge of the bed and tried to get down. He started to go headfirst, but that had been too scary, so he turned around and stuck his legs and little feet out the bed and tried to slide down it. However, he ended up hitting the floor and tumbling over onto his belly. Once there, my son knew that he had successfully made it out the bed, and took off crawling as fast as he could go.

My parents got a kick out of him climbing onto the living room couch. It was such a funny and joyful thing to see! They had never seen a baby that young successfully climb onto that green leather couch without any help. They told me that my son would place his big bubble head onto the couch, then try to sccot the rest of his body onto it. The first three tries were not successful, but on the fourth, he was able to place one knee onto the couch and thrust the rest of his body up there. Once he was seated on the couch, my son looked around the room as though he had just reached the top of a mountain.

"Can you imagine that?"

My son and I believe that not only single mothers, but single fathers, grandparents, or whoever is facing the challenging situation of raising boys with similar problems, can take something away from this book.

INTRODUCTION

This serious and heartfelt book by Daula Day is a must-read for single moms, or anyone with a troubled son. It illustrates the pain and agony our boys put us through when they choose to go down the wrong path. Once you pick this book up, you will not put it down!

In 1976, I was a single parent with four children: two boys and two girls. We lived in Baton Rouge, Louisiana. My first three kids' father never grew out of his teenage years and thug life. He believed it was cool to be a "Gangster." He used drugs & alcohol and physically abused me. At times, my son acted just like his father and I hated it! He had all of his father's ways and wanted to be just like him, but I was determined that my son would not follow in his footsteps.

This book, Got Out the Game, discusses my son's involvement with gangs, drug activity, alcohol abuse, and murder charges. It details the stress and sleepless nights I underwent raising a young black male and not losing him to the streets or the prison system. I elaborate on my son's childhood, teenage years, and adult life. There are far too many of our young men who are caught up in the game and never get out. This book was written to relate to all single mothers who are struggling with the same issues, or know someone in a similar situation.

CHAPTER 1

THE FATHER
ABSENT

DUMPLIN

My first three children's father was born in New Orleans. Everyone knew him as "Dumplin." He was approximately six feet, two inches tall, with a slender body frame. I was sixteen when I met Dumplin at a party in Rockwood, and twenty by the time we ended our relationship. It was a very stormy time with him. We fought constantly. At five feet, seven inches, and weighing about 120 pounds soaking wet, I was a small girl, but I would fiercely fight that son of a bitch back!

Dumplin did not spend much time with his children. However, he did spend some time with his son, Willie, who was known on the streets as "Willie Gat." The only other times my child saw his father in the neighborhood was on the corners drinking. My son did not take after his father's height. He was a short kid and only grew to be about five feet, nine inches tall, and had a slim body frame until adulthood. My little boy also had red nappy hair, and I do not know where he'd inherited it from.

Whenever Dumplin came and got Willie, he would let him sip beer and hang out with the other neighborhood thugs in Rockwood. He would give him a few dollars and tell him not to mention it to me because I would take the money from him if I knew he had it. That low-down, dirty dog had some nerve to tell my son something like that. However, Willie would come home and brag about the few dollars his father had given him. *Those stupid little funky dollars,* is what I thought to myself. Through no fault of theirs, Dumplin never came by to get his daughters. Call me foolish, but I never made Dumplin pay child support or pressured him to do anything for his children. I was determined to raise my kids the best I could without his help.

Willie grew up imitating his father, and this was something I did not appreciate. He would talk just like Dumplin, and even had his laugh. My son wanted everything his father had, from the gold tooth to the diamond earring. His father would always tell him that he would buy those things for him. Whenever Willie asked for a gold tooth and an earring, I angrily refused! I remember when he was a baby and able to eat solid food. I set him and his sister Renae at the kitchen table for breakfast. I prepared grits; it was one of their favorite meals. I placed the hot grits on the table and went to the refrigerator to get the butter. Before I could turn around, I heard a loud scream and frantic crying! When I rushed over to my baby to see what was wrong, he had hot grits on his face. He had somehow gotten to the grits, placed his fingers in the bowl, and tried to put the grits into his mouth. But he had missed, and the grits had landed on his face. The grits burned his face and left a permanent scar. That incident left me sad and upset for a very long time. I was dealing with two babies all alone, and their father was not there to help with his children. Every time I saw that scar on Willie's face, it just reminded me of that painful day, and that his father had not been there. It just broke my heart every time I saw that scar on my baby's face.

MOUNT ZION APARTMENTS

I used to drive an orange 1970s model Volkswagen Beetle that the kids called the "Dee Dee Bug." The Bug broke down on us a lot, but it always got us where we needed to go—eventually. The kids hated to ride in the Bug, fearing that it would break down and leave us stranded.

One night, the Bug broke down on us, and the kids got very scared. They all began to talk to one another like the characters on the 1970s show, *The Waltons*:

"Good night, John Boy."

"Good night, Mary Ellen."

Those children of mine were comical.

I was twenty-one years old when I moved out my parents' house with my three children, and rented a two-bedroom apartment located off I-110 and North 22nd Street. The area was called "Easy Town." I had to make several trips to get our stuff to the apartment, but eventually, we got it done. Our new place was at Mount Zion Apartments, which was located on the other side of town from my parents' home. It had two sections to it that faced one another within a sort of circular structure. One section had two floors, and the other section had three. My father told me to make sure that my apartment was not on the first floor, so we lived on the third. Thankfully, a church owned the apartments, and the rent was not high. The church made it their business to ensure that it stayed that way.

Times were tough for us back then, and the kids would make me real nervous wherever they came running into the apartments yelling,

"Free dryer!"

"Free dryer!"

Sometimes the dryer on one of the apartment floors would malfunction and spin for free for several hours. So the kids would run into the apartment, gather all the dirty clothes, and place them in the washer to take advantage of the dryer. Those children of mine were all over it, baby.

I loved my first apartment, but after seven years, the children thought we would never move, and started to get tired of it. All of them were cramped up together and sleeping in one room. They would always say:

"Mama, are we ever gonna move?"

"We will be the last people to leave these apartments."

"We have probably lived here longer than everybody else, and most of our friends have moved away!"

Easy Town was a rough part of Baton Rouge. There was a lot of gang activity, and the crime rate was high. In addition, some of the worst gangs that existed were members of a family. Every bad neighborhood in Baton Rouge had at least one family gang that lived there, and if one of their members had a fight, the rest of the family fought, too. Easy Town had the Spillards. The Mills and the Berds lived in South Baton Rouge: no one messed with those families without starting a war. However, I had to live where I could afford to, and no matter how bad things may have gotten, I would never let my kids see me worried or stressed. I showed very little emotion around them, and I felt pretty safe at Mount Zion Apartments. We had two huge maintenance men, Fred and Karl, who worked and lived at the apartment complex. They were muscular bodybuilders, and they always told me to let them know if I had any trouble. We also had a giant police officer name Mr. Earl Thompson as the apartment manager. He stood six feet, eight inches tall and weighed about 400 pounds. All of the neighborhood gangs in the area feared him.

One night, Dumplin showed up drunk at my apartment, banging on the door and demanding for me to open it and talk to him. It had been a year since we'd stopped dating, and I had nothing else to say to that bastard. My children's father was really crazy when he drank. He was known to act a donkey, in others words an ass, when he was loaded on drugs and alcohol. The banging woke up my youngest daughter, Monique, and she began to cry. I told her to get back in bed and not to follow me. She immediately ran back to bed. I was so scared that I went out to the balcony and thought about yelling out for help, but decided not to. Damn, the banging on door got louder it sounded like he was about to kick the door in. Oh shit, I had to do something right away; I couldn't let my kids see him beating on me. I looked over the balcony's rail and said to myself, "I can make it, I can climb all the way down to the bottom." And I did! I climbed down three stories, and ran to the manager's apartment to get Mr. Thompson. He returned with me to my apartment and looked around, but my children's father had left by then. Mr. Thompson told me to come and get him if Dumplin returned. I still do not know to this day how I was able to climb down that balcony. It had to be by the Grace of God! There was really nothing for me to hold onto. Thankfully, the kids' father never returned to the apartment again.

STRANGE MAN

My kids thought we were just fine regardless of how little we had, but raising four kids on a teacher's salary was very tough. I had to apply for welfare assistance, and got approved to receive food stamps. Willie hated to go grocery shopping with me. He was embarrassed to spend food stamps. Whenever I sent him to the corner store to purchase small food items, I had to give him real money. That little boy would not spend a food stamp to save his life.

One morning, I sent him to the corner store to buy a few things. The items he picked up cost more than the money I had given him. He was short a couple of bucks, but a man at the store paid the difference. My son returned home about thirty minutes later, and I could not believe what I saw: a bearded man had appeared in my bedroom! My mouth flew wide open, my heart dropped to my stomach, and my eyes almost popped out my head. He was a very tall, skinny man in filthy clothes. The man said in a deep, scratchy voice,

"Can you reimburse me the money I gave to your son?"

I tried to cover myself because I was still in my night-gown. I was so scared that I was shaking. I looked into my purse and saw that I had one twenty-dollar bill. I told Willie to go back to the store and get change, then give the man his money back and come straight home. After my son left the apartment, a horrific thought dawned on me: why would a strange man give a little boy money, never mind follow him home and enter his apartment?

Suddenly, I thought, *child molester.*

I immediately threw on a pair of jeans and my shoes, then ran out of the apartment, yelling for Willie. Once I reached my son, I asked him if the man had tried to do anything to him.

He replied, "Naw, Ma, that fool was not gonna get me!"

So I asked, "Why did you accept the man's money and then let him follow you home?"

I always told my children to put things back if they did not have enough money to pay for it.

My son told me that he had been trying to put things back, but the man had insisted on paying for it. Willie said that once he left the store, he had crossed the street to our apartments. He'd run very fast and thought that he had lost the man. My poor baby had to have been terrified!

My son said that he was just as surprised as I was that the man had followed him home and showed up in my bedroom.

I later reported that creepy man to Mr. Thompson and also told my father about the incident. Daddy told me he would speak with my son and also said, "Daula, you need a man in the house!"

Fortunately for the kids, the strange man was never seen again around the apartment complex.

CHAPTER 2

CHILDHOOD
CRITICAL TIME

LATCHKEY KIDS

Willie and my oldest daughter, Renae, grew up as "latchkey kids." They each wore a key around their necks and had responsibilities to do around the house when they got home from school. There were plenty of latchkey kids in our area at that time, and I had to threaten my son with the belt to finish all of his chores before he went outside and played with the other kids. I never prohibited my children from going outside to play after they completed their chores and schoolwork. We had no cable in the house, and a lot of their friends did, so Willie loved to go and watch television at his friend's house. I also had to restrict him from eating too many snacks; that boy would eat everything in the house, if you left it up to him. I had to limit that boy on how many snacks he could have a day. One of his favorite snacks was the Hostess Cupcake Ding Dong. He would eat the whole box of cupcakes, if I let him.

Renae grew up with a lot of responsibilities from an early age. She was in charge of cooking meals for the family when she got home from school. She began cooking in elementary school, around fourth or fifth grade. This was a big help to me, because the kids got home way before I did. Willie was responsible for taking out the trash, and making sure that the doors were locked before we all went to sleep at night. Both kids were responsible for cleaning the house. Sometimes Willie would forget to take the trash out, and I did not care how late it was—his butt was gonna take out the trash! I would go storming in the room, yelling at him and demanding that he take the trash out now!

He would respond, "Ma, it's real dark outside. Can I take the trash out in the morning?"

I would reply, "Hell, no!"

He would then say, "What if somebody kidnapped me?"

I would say to that little smart aleck. "Willie, nobody wants to kidnap your bad ass, now take that damn trash out right now before I get the belt!"

My son did not want to go down three flights of stairs and then outside to the dumpster late at night. However, he forgot to take the trash out a lot, and making him take the trash out regardless of the time of night was my only way of getting him to remember to do his job. The next day, Fred the maintenance man mentioned to me that someone was leaving trash behind the doors on the second floor. He found it really odd that someone was placing it behind the doors, as if to hide it. I never asked my son if he was the one putting trash behind the doors on the second floor, because he was finally taking the trash out on time, and I figured that he had learned his lesson. I was trying to raise him to grow up and be a responsible man. He liked to be called the man of the house, as my father had proclaimed him to be. Willie loved when Daddy told him that. He would stick his little chest out every time he heard him say it.

My son went through a spell where he did not want to go outside and play. One afternoon I asked him, "Boy, why haven't you been outside playing lately?"

He said, "Because I don't want the Atlanta Killer to catch me!"

I told him, "Boy, that man is all the way in Atlanta, now get your ass outside and play!"

Shortly after that, Willie explained to me that he had almost been kidnapped while walking home from a friend's house one day! He told me that a white van with three Caucasians inside had pulled up to him at the corner. A lady and a man were in the front seats; the side door to the van opened, and a creepy-looking white man inside asked him to come over and give him directions. Willie said that he took off quickly in the other direction.

My son said, "Ma, I was running so fast it could have been raining outside, and I wouldn't have even got wet."

I taught my children to never talk to strangers. I do not think that he made the story up to get back at me for making him go outside and play. I have never known my son to lie to me or make up stories. I reported the incident to the authorities in case another kid encountered the same thing.

PARK ELEMENTARY SCHOOL

My children attended Park Elementary School. It was walking distance from our apartment complex, and while they enjoyed going to that school, they did not like the extracurricular activities that occurred on and off campus. Willie explained how Darvin's gang would show up to their school during recess and torment the kids. They were a group of teenage guys who attended Capitol High School, which was located adjacent to my son's elementary school. The gang would appear out of nowhere and chase all the kids around the school. If the gang caught a kid, they would beat him up and take his snacks, shoes, backpack, and anything else in his possession. They would even take his money, if he had any. If the gang was not there terrorizing the children, the kids were constantly fighting one another. Almost every recess, there was a fight. My son had his share of fights at the school. I had to whip his butt all the time for receiving, "Behavior interferes with class work" on his report cards. I vigorously told him that he was going to school to get an education, not to be the class clown!

THE PUMPKIN

As a child, Willie would get into mischief like any other hardheaded kid. He did such things as breaking windows, knocking on apartment doors and running away before it was answered, fighting at school, and being disruptive in class. However, one thing he did surprised me. It was Halloween, and his teacher brought a pumpkin to class for the kids to make a jack-o'-lantern. She placed the pumpkin on a table near the pencil sharpener, and told the class that they would begin carving the pumpkin later, and that it was going to be so much fun. Willie looked around the classroom and saw the disappointed looks on the faces of his classmates, then raised his hand and asked the teacher if he could sharpen his pencil.

The teacher replied, "Why, certainly, child, you may sharpen your pencil."

After my son sharpened his pencil, he walked by the pumpkin and poked a small hole in it. The other kids watched him the entire time and thought this was very funny; later that day, someone else filled the whole pumpkin with pencil holes. When the teacher saw the punctured pumpkin, she burst out crying.

Then she said, "I can never do anything for you kids! You all do not appreciate anything!"

My son was sent to the principal's office and was blamed for punching all the holes in the pumpkin. He was very afraid, because the principal, Mr. Rocker, was known to give painful spankings with his huge wooden paddle.

However, that day Mr. Rocker did not paddle Willie, but instead gave him a verbal warning and harsh counseling. I told my boy that that had been a horrible thing to do. Why had he done it?

My son replied, "Cuz, we didn't want no stupid pumpkin; all the kids in the other classrooms got candy for Halloween. They were teasing and charming us with their miniature pumpkin candies.""So, I, umm, just got mad and poked the pumpkin one time.""Someone else had punched the other holes and lied on me, so he or she would not get in trouble."

My son told me that he was very upset and disappointed about the pumpkin-carving idea. He later explained that the kids in the class had not wanted a pumpkin, either. They had all wanted candy for Halloween, like their friends had gotten in the other classrooms. It was later revealed that a girl had punched the other holes in the pumpkin. She was a girl who everyone in the class had picked on for being ugly, stinky, and dirty, and she did not have a single friend in the class.

I did not whip my son for that incident, but for the most part, whenever he got into trouble, I beat him vigorously with the belt. There were times when I beat him so badly that my parents had to pull me off him.

As I beat his butt, I would shout to him, "You are not gonna be like your damn father!"

I would repeat those words to him over and over again. I did not like whipping my son, but I was determined that he would not be like his father.

WILLIE'S FIRST BOOK

My son was always a smart child; he wrote a book in the second grade at Park Elementary School. It won first place in the school's book contest, and he was asked to read the book before parents, faculty, and students during the school's graduation ceremony. It was a big event, and both of my parents attended. When the curtains opened, and the teacher introduced Willie, he walked slowly onto the stage with his head down, clutching his book tightly with one hand as he approached the podium. After reaching the podium, my son paused for several minutes. Then hesitantly raised his head and scanned the room until he spotted Daddy sitting in the audience. I guess my father relaxed my son's nerves, because Willie began to read once he saw him. I can still picture my son opening the book and saying in a clear kid's voice, *"King of the Jungle,* by Willie Day." In the book, Willie stated each animal's case for being king of the jungle, and of course the lion made the strongest argument and won the title. It was one of the proudest moments in my life as a mother to see my little boy on stage reading his book. After he finished, the audience gave him thunderous applause and a standing ovation. I kept that book for over thirty years, and the kids in my classrooms loved to read it. It was the first book the kids ran to read in my classroom.

THE BIG WHEEL RACE

The summers were when the kids had the most fun, and racing one another was one of the main competitive events. I enjoyed watching the races from my bedroom window. I recall the Big Wheel race. I had bought Willie a Big Wheel that he kept for many years. My son wanted one of the new Green Machines that had come out, but I could not afford it. However, he was fine with that because my boy still loved his Big Wheel: it was very durable and fast.

He would yell to my bedroom window from the playground below, "Ma, throw down my Big Wheel."

Our apartment was located on the third floor, facing the playground area. I would toss that Big Wheel over the balcony, and it would slam to the ground and tumble to a complete stop without a dent.

Ron, another kid in the apartment complex who had just gotten a new Green Machine for the summer, challenged Willie to race. All the kids were yelling and pumping up for the big race. No one had ever beaten my son in a race with his Big Wheel. The track was a wide concrete sidewalk that was positioned around the bowl-shaped field where the kids from the apartment complex liked to play.

As the kids got into position, the older kids said, "Go!"

Willie and Ron took off down the sidewalk.

Some kids would yell,

"Green Machine!"

"Green Machine!"

The other kids would yell,

"Big Wheel!"

"Big Wheel!"

As they pedaled up a gentle incline, my son started to pump his legs faster, and separated from the Green Machine. I'd never seen his little legs move that fast before; he was determined to win that race. Once they made the first turn, Willie began to pull away from the Green Machine and left it behind. When he made it to the finish line, he jumped up and down, and kept yelling,

"Big Wheel!"

"Big Wheel!"

"Big Wheel!"

A few months later, the Big Wheel was stolen. My son was very angry and upset. It was probably the best toy that I had ever bought him. He told me that he hoped God would strike down the thief for taking his Big Wheel. I told him not to wish ugly things like that on anyone.

DREW

Unlike my first three children's father, my youngest son, Gerrod, had quite a different dad. His name was Drew. He was originally from Baton Rouge, but had moved away early on in his childhood to New York City, and had spent some time in Chicago. Therefore, he did not speak with a southern accent, but spoke very properly, and Willie enjoyed imitating Drew. His favorite imitation was of Drew placing his regular breakfast order at McDonald's. My son would mock Drew and say, "Yes, could I please have two Egg McMuffin sandwiches and two orange juices."

We all would crack up because Willie could sound just like him. The kids would die laughing because they never ordered the Egg McMuffin sandwiches for breakfast at McDonald's.

Unlike Dumplin's family, Drew's people spent time with Gerrod. Drew also did some fatherly things with Willie: he often took my son hunting and to work with him. Drew enjoyed taking my son to work. Willie did exactly what Drew instructed him to do, and did not stop working until it was time to break for lunch or go home. Willie was still a little kid, so Drew would have him assist with small things, such as placing putty in the holes in the walls, fetching tools, and cleaning buckets. Drew had his own business as a commercial and residential painter, and he also performed home remodeling. Gerrod was too small at the time to go on any of the hunting and working trips.

Willie looked forward to the hunting trips. He would get his hunting clothes out the night before and be outside before the sun came up, waiting for Drew to pick him up from the apartment. They would leave very early in the morning to hunt raccoons and sometimes wild turkeys. Drew would bring his coon dogs, rifles, and hunting gear for the trip. Willie enjoyed those hunting trips, especially when the dogs were hot on a raccoon's trail. The raccoon would go from tree to tree, and Drew would flash a light in the tree to spot the raccoon. The raccoon would then cover its eyes to not give away its position.

There was one thing that my son persistently asked Drew to do for him, but which Drew would always refuse. It was karate: Willie wanted Drew to teach him martial arts. Willie saw Drew as fearless, especially when he witnessed Drew go face-to-face with a very large man named Big John. Big John stood about six feet, four inches tall, and weighed about 250 pounds. Drew was about five feet, nine inches even, and weighed about 175 pounds. They were toe-to-toe, discussing some work Drew had done at Big John's house for which Big John was refusing to pay.

Drew told Big John, "I completed all the work that you requested in a timely manner, and you are going to pay me right now, mister!"

Drew pointed his finger to the ground as he demanded that Big John pay up. Big John backed down and produced the cash from his pocket. My son reenacted the entire scene and had us all falling out laughing as he imitated Drew.

Drew was a black belt in karate, and Willie wanted badly to learn. He had asked me to enroll him in karate classes, but I could not afford to.

Every time he asked Drew to teach him karate, Drew would respond, "Why do you want to learn karate?"

Willie would say, "Because it's fun."

Drew would tell my son that that was not the correct answer. I think my boy started to try and figure out the answer Drew wanted to hear when he asked him that question.

So the next time Drew asked him, "Why do you want to learn karate?"

Willie got slick and said, "For protection!"

Drew replied, "Protection from whom?"

My son said, "From the bad guys."

Then Drew laughed and said, "No, you want to learn it so you can whip other boys and impress the girls. That is not what karate is used for, and I will teach you when I think you are ready."

One time, after a hunting trip, Drew captured a raccoon and kept it in a cage at his house. Willie was over visiting one day and Drew told him not to mess with that raccoon. Willie wondered why Drew would say that, because the raccoon just sat in the cage and was very calm and still. When Drew went into the house, Willie got a stick and slowly poked at the raccoon. My son said that after he poked the raccoon, it charged the cage and grabbed it with its claws. Then it rattled the cage real loud, hissing and showing its sharp teeth, and all the raccoon's fur was standing up. Willie told me that he dropped the stick and immediately ran into the house, his heart pounding, gasping for air. Drew came out laughing and said, "Boy, I told you not to mess with that raccoon."

That was not the first time Willie's curiosity had gotten him into trouble. During their hunting trips, Drew liked to chew tobacco. Willie asked Drew if he could chew some tobacco, too. Drew told him that he was too young to chew tobacco. Then Drew said, "Okay, I will give you only a little bit, but do not swallow it." My son placed the tobacco behind his lower lip exactly where Drew put his. Every so often, he would spit the tobacco juice out just like Drew did. Abruptly, Drew told Willie to stay put while he went to check something out in the woods. However, when Drew walked out of Willie's sight for several minutes, my son decided to see what would happen if he swallowed just a little bit of the tobacco juice. Willie said that shortly after he swallowed some of the tobacco juice, the woods around him started spinning. Then he felt sick to his stomach and threw up his breakfast on the ground. When Drew returned, he began to laugh and said, "Boy, I told you not to swallow it. One day you are gonna learn to listen."

My son did not have birthday celebrations as a kid, but Drew would sometimes purchase toys for him. However, some of these toys would be ones that Drew enjoyed more for himself, like an electric train set, and a model car that took a lot of skill to operate or build.

These toys were a little too advanced for my son, and he did not play with them much. So he traded his model car set for a pair of football shoulder pads from an older kid in the apartment complex.

Drew did a lot of positive things with my son and Willie appreciated everything. However, Drew was tragically shot and killed at a nightclub event. The incident was shocking to my son Willie, and had a major impact on my youngest boy, Gerrod. Drew was only thirty-six years old.

CHAPTER 3

THE NEPHEW
PARTNER IN CRIME

MIKE BLACK

My sister Belle's son, Mike Black, was born five months after Willie. They were pretty much raised as brothers, and you rarely saw one without the other. They loved to play and watch football together all the time. My son was a diehard New Orleans Saints fan, and my nephew was a faithful Dallas Cowboys fan. The two of them would play football from sunup to sundown with the other kids in the area. Willie and Mike Black were pretty good football players, and all the young boys enjoyed playing football with them. They were very competitive in everything they did. They would get all into playing football to the point where their socks and towels had to be folded a certain way. They would always ask my sister and me to buy them football uniforms with helmets, shoulder pads, cleats, and all the rest of that football gear, which my sister and I could not afford. The closest my son came to a football uniform was a jersey with his name on the back. He loved that jersey and wore it with pride.

My son and nephew had been getting into things together since they wore diapers, especially when a fight occurred. Any fight that Mike Black had, Willie believed was his fight, too. Whenever we were over visiting my sister, Willie and Mike Black would discuss fights that they had had with other boys. Mike Black told my son how these two boys ganged up on him, and I heard my son say, "We gon' get them fools tomorrow." I told my son to stop discussing fights or his butt was going back home with me. Nevertheless, Willie and Mike Black would find those boys and beat them down. The older kids who lived in my sister's apartment complex liked when Willie visited Mike Black because they could stir up fights between my son and a guy with whom Mike Black had previously had a fight. There was this one big kid named Bear who sort of looked like a man-child. The older boys from the area began to pick a fight between my son and Bear. They told Willie that Bear had messed over Mike Black after playing football one day. Then Bear began to try to bully Willie. My son said that he hauled off and punched Bear in his nose, and it started bleeding heavily! He then swiftly got into his fighting stance and told Bear, "Punk, come on with it!"

However, Bear did not. Instead, he ran home crying to his mama. My son always had to fight, and would send most boys home with bloody noses, black eyes, and busted lips. Their parents would show up at my sister's or my apartment, complaining about how my son had beaten their child, but never about how their child had started it. Willie and Mike Black were fighting the boys they played with all the time. There was another kid named Joon who had to be twice as big as my son, and he would come knocking on my door all the time, saying that Willie had beaten him up. He came by so often that I knew who it was before I even opened the door.

COUSIN'S WEDDING

I remembered the time my sister and I dressed our sons alike for our cousin's wedding. The boys were no more than seven or eight years old. We bought them these beautiful light-blue-and-gold suits. I recall hearing the boys say, "Man, these are some bad suits, and the shirts look really shiny and slippery." Little did I know why they were so impressed by the shiny, slippery shirts; I soon found out, when they were both covered in dirt. Those two boys held a contest in the reception's hallway: they wanted to see who could run down the hall and slide the farthest. They were having so much fun sliding down the hallway that several other kids joined in on the competition. My son may have had fun sliding on the floor, but I'd paid good money for that suit, and he knew better than to behave that way, especially in public. I tore his butt up real good when we got home that day!

MUD BALLS

It was the summer of 1979, and trouble seemed to always find the boys around this time. There was an incident that involved Willie, Mike Black, and some other boys in our apartment complex. On rainy days when the ground

was saturated, the boys would make mud balls, stand at a
second floor window near the street, and take turns
throwing mud balls at passing vehicles. Those mud balls
made a very loud thump when they struck a vehicle. One
particular time, some mud balls hit the wrong man's
vehicle. Once the mud balls made an impact, the man
immediately slammed on his brakes, got out of his shiny,
red Ford Mustang, and ran into the apartment complex
after the boys. All of the boys frantically scrambled away
from the window and ran to their homes. Later, I got a
knock on my door from an angry, heavily breathing black
man who told me about the mud balls that had hit his
Mustang. The man implicated my son and nephew.
Willie was behind me, listening to the entire conversation, and heard the man tell me that he had spoken with
the lady who lived in the apartment right below me, and
that her son had mentioned that my kids had been the
ones throwing mud balls. Once Willie heard that, he
eased away to hide his belt. I asked the man if his Mustang had been damaged.

He said, "No, just muddy, but someone could have
been seriously injured. This foolishness has to stop!"

I told the man that my son and nephew most likely had
not hit his car with the mud balls. However, they had

probably been there when the incident had occurred, because they played with all the boys in the apartment complex. I assured the man that this matter would be looked into, and apologized to him for the incident. After the furious gentleman left my door, I yelled for Willie and Mike Black.

My son approached me and said, "Aww, Ma, they lying on us. It was the boys downstairs below our apartment that hit the man's vehicle with the mud balls. They are just saying that to save themselves!"

My blood was boiling by this time, and I did not want to hear anything else about what had happened. I told that little joker that he and Mike Black should not have been there at all; they knew better than to get into trouble and hang around it. I immediately went to get the belt, but could not find it, and told my son, "I know you hid it, and when I find it, your butt is mine."

I looked all over for that belt. I decided to check one more place where I thought he might have hidden it. I found it under the bed, tucked between the box springs. I must have whipped them for an hour straight, and later took Mike Black home. I made Willie stay inside until I got tired of looking at his nappy, redheaded ass, and did not allow Mike Black to stay over again for months. This was another way of punishing my son, since the two of them were very close. He and his cousin were like brothers, and were the best of friends. Their fathers had grown up as buddies, and you rarely saw one without the other. They both ran the streets together, and remained friends all their lives.

The majority of the time, I visited my sister's home. Mike Black asked if he could stay at my house for the weekend. I told him, "No, maybe next weekend," because Mike Black had just spent the previous weekend at my place, and if it were left up to him, he would choose to stay every weekend with us. By the time we left my sister's house, everyone was tired. The drive home was in complete silence. And just as I pulled into the apartment driveway, Mike Black popped his head up from behind the back seat, where the kids had hidden him. That boy was a sneaky little rascal. They all burst out laughing. He had to stay, because I was not about to drive him all the way back to my sister's house. They played this game on me all the time. Mike Black would end up staying with us for weeks at a time. This was not good. The boys really needed to spend some time away from one another; the both of them got into too much trouble together.

THE PATIO

There was another incident during the summer when Willie, Mike Black, and their friend, Lil' D, were throwing rocks at a wasp nest near a glass patio. Unexpectedly, I received a knock on my door from the apartment management, who told me to replace a glass patio window. They said that another tenant and her son, Lil' D, who had been playing with my son and nephew earlier that day, had reported that my son had thrown a rock and busted the window. Willie explained to me that neither his rock nor Mike Black's rock had hit the window. Lil' D's rock had hit the window, but the window had not broken.

It was determined that the rain that had occurred later that day caused the window to shatter. For some reason, I believed my son that time, and was probably tired from wearing his butt out over the mud balls. I knew that because we were poor, the kids got bored and made up things to do. Sadly, I did not have the money to enroll them in camps and keep them occupied.

FREE POOL

However, one summer, I was able to enroll my son in part-time swimming lessons, though I could not afford a full membership for him. Of course, Willie wanted Mike Black to take the lessons, too. Willie's friend, Mo' Money, also signed up for the class. They really enjoyed the swimming classes, and after each class was over, the kids would sneak into the members-only pool and swim some more. The children called it the "free pool." This pool was for full-time members who knew how to swim, and lifeguards were not on duty. One scary incident occurred when my sister Belle brought two of her other boys, Squirk and Hoss, to swim in the "free pool." Squirk was seven years old, and Hoss was six; neither boy knew how to swim. On this occasion, Squirk wandered off into a deeper part of the pool. Suddenly, he disappeared.

Oh my God, Squirk was drowning!

Fortunately, my boy had been keeping an eye on him the whole time he was in the pool. Willie knew that Squirk was a hardhead and required extra attention. When my son saw him go under and not come back up, he quickly swam over to him and pulled him out of the water. Willie saved Squirk's life that day. Everyone was shaken, but relieved and thankful for what my son had done. Willie thought nothing of it because he always looked after all the younger kids in the family: as the oldest grandson in our family of eighteen grandkids he considered it his responsibility to do so. Belle was overjoyed that her son had not drowned in the pool. But as a result, the kids never swam in the "free pool" again.

SUMMER CAMP

School was out, and I enrolled Willie and Mike Black in a free summer camp sponsored by Southern University. The camp utilized Southern's facilities and exposed the kids to a lot of different things. Youngsters from all over Baton Rouge attended the camp; Renae was even able to get a summer job there. I thought that this would be a great way to keep the boys out of trouble and give them something to do during the summer. Besides, it would keep their minds occupied. The camp offered all kinds of fun activities, such as swimming, basketball, football, mentoring, and weight lifting, and it also provided meals. I think the kids must have attended camp for maybe two weeks before they began to skip and hang out at the neighborhood park. Word got back to me that they were hanging out at the park until camp ended, and then returning home. This made me very angry because the summertime was when kids got into a lot of trouble with the free time they had off from school. Their reason for skipping camp was, "It was too hot outside."

CHAPTER 4

THE GRANDFATHER
FATHER FIGURE

DADDY

In 1978, I had to take a teaching job out of town, and my kids had to live with relatives until I got settled. Willie begged me to let him stay with my sister, Belle, so that he and Mike Black could go to school together. I agreed to let him stay there and attend school with my nephew. One morning, as Willie got dressed for school at around 6:30 a.m., he heard a loud knock at the door. His aunt, Belle, went to the door, and Willie stood in the hall to see who was there. Then my son heard a familiar voice and knew who it was right away: it was my father, telling Belle to have Mann pack all of his things because he was going to live with him and attend school in Rockwood. "Mann" was the nickname that Daddy had given my son. Belle tried to tell our father that I wanted my son to stay with her, but he did not want to hear another word about it. My son was devastated. He had been looking forward to having so much fun going to school with Mike Black and staying at his aunt's house. Later, my son appreciated living with my parents because he was able to concentrate on his schoolwork.

Daddy was a great role model and a positive influence in my boy's life. My son admired, respected, and loved my father very much. He saw my dad as his own father figure. Daddy inspired Willie to write his first book, *King of the Jungle*. He loved to tell my son stories about the animals in the jungle, with the lion as the king of them all. My son would sit there in suspense, his eyes and mouth wide as Daddy vividly described the scenes.

My father was known to give his kids a good butt-whipping whenever they got out of line, but he never whipped my son. However, one day, Daddy had gotten fed up with him and Mike Black. They had been getting on Daddy's last nerve all day. It started early that morning with the boys having a so-called "china ball war." They had these little green balls all over the car porch from shooting at one another. My son and Mike Black would pick the little balls from the neighbor's china ball tree for their combat games. They would cut a six- or seven-inch piece of a small-diameter water hose, and partially shave a stick to slide it back and forth inside the hose. This little homemade gun could launch a china ball a nice distance. Willie and Mike Black each had a gun and a pouch full of china balls. Sometimes their friends joined in on the fun with their own homemade china ball guns. When Daddy saw all those china balls all over his car porch, he had a fit and immediately made them clean up the mess. He told them to play somewhere else with those china balls. Willie and Mike Black continued to play more games, but inside the house, where they began to horse around with one another. Daddy did not tolerate children playing in the house. He warned them twice to cut it out and go outside. However, they kept playing around in the house, and broke Mama's beautiful vase.

When Daddy heard that vase hit the floor and shatter, he yelled, "Mann and Mike Black, I told y'all assholes to stop playing in the got-damn house, and now both of your butts belong to me!"

When those two boys heard my father coming quickly toward them, they took off running outside. They hid behind the house and watched Daddy from there, their hearts beating fast!

My father walked around the house with his big, black, leather belt, yelling, "Mann and Mike Black, y'all better not run from me!"

The boys ran to the other end of the house as Daddy began to walk toward them. They watched him the entire time and manage to stay out of his sight. They continued to run around the house until Daddy got tired of looking for them. Those boys had never been whipped by my father before, but they heard how painful the beatings could be. They managed to escape that day, but never did anything else to upset Daddy ever again.

My father spent as much time as he could with my son. He convinced my boy that he was the man of the house at seven years old. My father would take Willie to the family's garden and teach him how to plant and harvest crops. He taught Willie how to fish with a reel, and dig worms from the ground for bait. I still remember the day my son caught his first fish and brought it home in a bucket to show everyone: he had caught a nice-sized shoepick, and my father made him feel as though he had caught the biggest fish in the pond. My son was so proud of himself that day. Daddy also let him mow the lawn at a very young age; Willie's head barely cleared the lawn mower's bars, and his arms stretched out as far as they could go, but he used his legs to push the mower forward with all of his might.

Willie would mow the entire front yard without stopping, then say to my father, "Daddy, I cut the whole front yard and I am not even tired."

My father would say, "Go on, Mann, you did a good job!"

My father would then get him started on mowing the backyard. Daddy would also take him grocery shopping, and challenged Willie to calculate the prices in his head. Daddy had been told about the incident where Willie had been short of money, and a strange man had paid the difference and followed him home. My father wanted to make sure that Willie never came up short at the checkout counter again. The training ground was the local grocery store. Daddy told Willie to round each item's price up to the nearest dollar amount. After several items had been placed in the grocery cart, he asked my son to tell him the total cost. Once they reached the checkout counter and were given the total amount owed, Willie was right on the money with his calculations. My son was very good at math; it was his favorite subject. He also made the advanced reading team in elementary school. He would rush home from school to do his homework before he went out to play with his friends. In class, he always turned in his homework even when his friends did not. He laughed about this because he always enjoyed to "one-up" his friends. He got a kick out of staying ahead of them in everything.

My parents' house was an average single-family home with three bedrooms, one bathroom, a kitchen, and a big backyard. The house was about 1,500 square feet, and we had a big family. When Willie lived there, my parents were in the process of making an addition to the house. This included a large den, utility room, remodeled kitchen, and a second bathroom. Willie loved to help with the construction for the house. He worked on whatever my father needed him to do. One task he enjoyed was chipping the mortar from the old bricks with a hammer and chisel. My son would be at it all day until there were no bricks left.

CHAPTER 5

THE UNCLES
ROLE MODELS

BIG UNC

While living with my parents, Willie got to spend a lot of time with his uncles. One of my younger brothers, who the children called "Big Unc," bought my son his first skateboard and taught him how to ride a bike. He also explained the game of football to him. It was my son's favorite sport; he enjoyed playing football and watching it on television all the time. He would watch football from morning to night as a little boy. My brother was arguably the greatest high school football running back ever in the state of Louisiana, and my son admired and feared him. My brother's photo and plaque were still displayed in his high school's locker room when my kids were enrolled. He had received all kinds of prestigious trophies and awards for running track and playing football; his touchdowns were shown on the local sports news highlights. He was so fast and elusive that his teammates gave him the nickname "Gray Ghost," and his motto was, "Now you see me, and now you don't." Our entire family just knew he was destined to play professional football. The head coach of Grambling State University, the legendary Eddie Robinson, personally came to my parents' house to recruit my brother. There was a number of other big-name football schools, such as Notre Dame, that were also interested in him. He received a full scholarship and played college football at a major local university. My brother told me years later that the head coach at that school had wanted a percentage of the money should he make it to the NFL. My brother refused, and the coach significantly reduced his playing time. I think that pretty much ended my brother's quest to play professional football, which confused and devastated our family.

Big Unc married his high school sweetheart, Fae, and they had three sons: Andy, Ron, and Brandon. My brother did the right thing by keeping his boys off the streets, out of Rockwood, and away from hard drugs and alcohol. Today, Andy is a minister, Don is a writer, and Brandon is a dentist, and they are all happily married. According to my son, Fae is the best cook in the whole world. She can cook just about anything, and her desserts are some of the very best. We all loved when she made old-fashioned, homemade ice cream. It was so delicious! We all would take turns turning the ice cream with the hand crank while Fae instructed everyone on what to next. It was a lot of fun making homemade ice cream, and the kids really enjoyed it. However, when Willie got into trouble as a kid, I would threaten him by saying, "I am gonna call Big Unc." His uncle was six feet, two inches tall with a muscular build, and was very mean. Willie would instantly plead for me not to call him. He would straighten up for about a week, but be back to his usual self after that.

❖ ❖ ❖

One time, Willie had a fight with another kid named KJ from the neighborhood, and beat him pretty badly. They were fighting over a playful rock-throwing incident that had gotten out of hand. KJ's neighbors, G. Tony and Melaki, were two older teenagers who did not like the fact that KJ had lost the fight with Willie. So they staged another fight between my son and KJ. However, this time they brought KJ's brother, "Big Craig." They all waited for my son to walk home from elementary school one day, then let KJ and Big Craig double-team him. My son's friend, Lil' Boonie, was with him and tried to help, but G. Tony and Melaki held him back. When Willie arrived home, Big Unc noticed that he had a bloody nose and a busted lip.

Big Unc asked, "What happened?"

Willie explained that two older boys had let two brothers double-team him and had held Lil' Boonie back from helping.

Big Unc asked for the names of the older boys, and Willie told him, "G. Tony and Melaki."

Big Unc told my son that he would get them!

Maybe a month or two passed, and no one saw G. Tony or Maleki around the neighborhood. One afternoon, Willie was playing in the front yard of my parents' house when G. Tony and Melaki rode by on their bicycles. Willie looked up and saw Big Unc walk outside the house and spot the two boys. When G. Tony and Melaki saw Big Unc staring them down, they immediately took off pedaling as fast as they could. My son had never seen his uncle run, but heard how fast he had been on the football field. Willie said that Big Unc ran by him in a blur, and caught the two teenagers down the street. Willie heard them hollering from hundreds of yards away, begging and pleading for Big Unc not to hit them again.

Willie heard Big Unc say, "You better not ever fool with my nephew again!" while beating them with his huge fists.

All of Willie's uncles were very protective of him, and so was his dad. However, Big Unc was known to beat up the neighborhood thugs who tried to harm his nephews. My brothers told Willie to never back down to anyone, but if the guy were much older than him, he ought to let them know so they could handle it.

LC

LC, my youngest brother, lived with us at times, and constantly played around with his nephew. My son would laugh, mock, and mess with his uncle all the time. However, LC would catch my boy and body-punch him for doing it. LC was my son's gangster uncle who was known on the streets as "ICE MAN." My son liked to imitate his uncle. My brother was known to have the best set of hands in Rockwood, and to not back down to anyone. He was left-handed, real quick, and he hit very hard. My little boy would watch him slap box other guys in the neighborhood, and was amazed at how no one could get a lick on his uncle. LC also had the biggest gun and the toughest dogs in the neighborhood; he owned a .44 Magnum pistol, or as Dirty Harry put it, "the most powerful handgun in the world," and often expressed that to his nephew.

My son used that gun to kill someone later in his life.

My brother also had a small derringer pistol, and Mike Black almost shot Willie while playing with it one day. They were both around twelve or thirteen years old when the frightening incident occurred. They were in my son's bedroom, ironing clothes to wear to the mall.

Willie told Mike Black, "Hey, I know where ICE MAN keeps his derringer pistol."

Mike Black said, "What's a derringer?"

"It's a very small gun that can fit in your fist."

Mike Black replied, "Dang, where's it at? I want to check it out, I never seen one of those before!"

Willie said, "It's under the mattress."

Mike Black got the gun from under the mattress. He started fooling around with the gun's hammer, and it went off. The bullet went through the bed right next to where my son was ironing his clothes!

Fortunately, no one was shot!

After that incident, my brother did not bring his guns into the house ever again. Willie was shaken for a while, and still could not believe what had happened. He and Mike Black were in shock for the next couple of weeks.

Following that incident, I must have double-checked the rooms several times a day to make sure no guns had been left in the house. I just could not get the thought out of my head that one of them could have been killed or seriously injured.

SLICK

My oldest brother, whom everyone called "Slick," would talk to Willie all the time. Slick was a consultant to the boys in our family; he could discuss anything with my son on any level, at any time. Slick and Willie would spend hours at a time discussing things that occurred in Rockwood. He constantly told my son to always watch his back and never let his guard down.

Rockwood was a very close-knit community: everyone in the neighborhood knew one another, and one could go to anyone's barbecue cookout, grab a plate of food, drink, and socialize without an invitation to do so. Our neighbors even babysat Willie for me when I was in college. The neighborhood was not very large, and consisted of approximately three to four hundred people. However, it was a hotspot for drug activity: people came through Rockwood around the clock to score dope. There was drama happening there all the time. Fights, shootings, stabbings, burglaries, and killings occurred frequently. Someone was always getting his head busted in the streets. I don't recall it being that bad back in my day, but the neighborhood just got worse over time.

Slick also loved to drink beer and listen to rap music with the boys. He was up on the hottest rap artists and their songs. He enjoyed laughing and joking around with Willie, Mike Black, and their homeboys. Slick was what the boys referred to as the "kicking it uncle."

DOG MAN

And then there was my sister Belle's husband, "Dog Man," who was a retired Vietnam veteran. He had received all kinds of awards for his service in the Army. Dog Man had been awarded a Purple Heart Medal during his combat in Vietnam. However, his name had no relationship to him being a dog breeder or dog lover: he was as mean and tough as a Rottweiler. There were times when guys would knock on my sister's door for Dog Man to walk them home because some gang members with guns were nearby, waiting to squabble with them.

Dog Man would yell for Belle to grab his pistol, and he would tell the guys, "Don't worry about those little punks, I will walk with you."

Dog Man was a very strict disciplinarian. He told me to call him any time I had trouble with my son, and that he did not mind if my boy stayed the entire summer with him. Willie loved to stay at their house, but only when

Dog Man was not there. The only time he and Mike Black were happy to see Dog Man was late at night on the weekends, when Dog Man would come home with hot Krispy Kreme doughnuts. Willie said that those doughnuts were delicious, and Dog Man knew that the boys would be up waiting just to see if he had bought them. Sometimes if Dog Man did not bring the dough-nuts, he would have Belle make breakfast; she would cook thick bacon slices, eggs, and biscuits with syrup for everyone. It did not matter if it was 1:00 a.m. or 5:00 a.m.—Belle was cooking breakfast for everyone.

Dog Man was hard on Willie and Mike Black. When Dog Man first met my sister, Mike Black had been a little boy; Belle later had five kids by Dog Man: two boys and three girls. Dog Man routinely screamed them down like a drill sergeant. He constantly yelled, worked, and talked harshly to the boys. He would have them clean his van inside and out in the blazing heat. Whenever Dog Man's nephew, Keyno, came over, Dog Man did not cut him any slack, either. He put Keyno right outside with Willie and Mike Black to help with the van. Then, once they were finished, the boys had to make sure that all the paper was picked up from the front and backyard. Dog Man stayed on those rascals, and they needed it.

Sometimes, Dog Man got extreme when he laughed about how worthless my son and nephew dads were, and called them by their dads' nicknames: Lil' Dumplin and Lil' Ruboo. He told them whenever he went to visit Belle during their earlier dating days; he would see their wine-head daddies standing on the corner, drinking in Rock-wood.

To avoid Dog Man, my son and nephew would get up early in the morning and leave the house. They would not return home until Dog Man left for work later that day. When Dog Man was not there, everything was great! Belle let the boys have all kinds of fun: they got to play, invite friends over, watch television, go places, stay up late, snack on whatever, and do whatever they wanted, too. They especially liked when Keyno came over to stay during the summers. Keyno was a few years older than Willie and Mike Black. Whenever Keyno was there, he turned up the fun. He would discuss having sex with girls, and make up all kinds of crazy games to play. One game he loved to play was "mustard mouth." The first person between the three of them who fell asleep would get mustard put in his mouth. My son said that it was so funny to see one of them smacking on mustard while he was asleep, then wake to realize he had mustard in his mouth and that everyone was laughing at him. Some-times, if none of them fell asleep, Keyno would get one of the two younger boys, Squirk or Hoss, with the mustard mouth. It was the best place a kid could spend his summer. Belle never fussed or yelled, and hardly ever whipped them. I do remember that she whipped them one time because Willie and Mike Black had a fight over a basketball game. Willie asked his aunt why she whipped him harder than she whipped her own son; she told him because he was the oldest and should know better. Furthermore, they should never fight one anoth-er, and should look after each other instead. This is something Willie really believed and lived by. He would take up for his cousin all the time, and looked out for him as they grew up. Whatever Willie had, he would try to provide for Mike Black. Willie later got Mike Black his first job as a busboy at the Italian restaurant where he worked. They did everything together, and spent most of their adolescent lives with each other.

COOLEY AND RAY

My children's father, Dumplin, had two brothers named Cooley and Ray; they were good guys, but they were estranged uncles to Willie and my daughters. Cooley and Ray only spoke to Willie when they saw him in the streets. My son would see them every now and then, when he was out playing in the neighborhood, or when he visited Dumplin's mother, who was a very frank lady. She would tell you exactly what was on her mind, and held nothing back. Willie was the only one of my children who would go over to her house to visit. The older of his two uncles, Cooley, was a very laid-back and mellow guy. He greeted my son with a warm "Kool-Aid" smile every time he saw him. Cooley loved to sing, dance, and drink his alcohol. Ray was Dumplin's younger brother, and a pretty big man. He was six foot one and weighed 220 pounds. Ray had played college football at Nicholls State University, and had been selected into the 1985 National Football League Draft in the fourth round as a defensive back by the Cincinnati Bengals. He had also played for the Pittsburgh Steelers. Ray was a quiet guy with a kind heart. I remember him having to meet me halfway to his mother's house to carry Willie. My son was a very large baby with a big head, and was too heavy for me to carry by myself.

CHAPTER 6

CHILDHOOD FRIEND
BORN HUSTLER

MO' MONEY

My son had a childhood friend whom we called "Mo' Money" because he was the only kid who walked around our neighborhood with a pocket full of change all the time. Mo' Money did not live in Mount Zion Apartments, but he played there every day. If my son was not playing in the apartment complex, he was over at Mo' Money's house. I let him go over there and play because Mo' Money's lived nearby. I had also met Mo' Money's mom, Beth, and she was a very nice lady; whenever my son was at their house, she treated him like her very own son. She took Willie to the store with Mo' Money to purchase school supplies for both of our sons, which was a very kind thing for her to do, and when I offered to pay her back, she refused. Mo' Money loved to play football with Willie and the other boys who lived in the apartment complex. They played in the grass field between the two apartment sections, where they used the circular drainage inlet at each end to represent the touchdown areas. Willie always complained about the change in Mo' Money's bulging pockets, which hurt the boys' hands whenever they tried to tackle him.

Mo' Money was a tall, slim, red-complexioned boy the same age as my son. They had met in Head Start and became lifelong friends. He and my son constantly looked for ways to get paid. Willie and Mo' Money would go door to door at the apartment complex and empty trash for money. They would also collect aluminum cans and walk about one-and-a-half miles to the recycling yard to sell them. The recycling yard paid them based on the collective weight of the cans they had collected. Willie and Mo' Money were always hustling to get paid. Sometimes the boys bought cheeseburgers at the local Corner Café with the cash they got from the aluminum cans. The Corner Café was for adults only, but the owner took a liking to the boys and let them eat there, anyway. Another place his little butt did not belong was in the pool hall. Children had no business being in those types of establishments, but if Mo' Money was in the pool hall, my son was there too.

Those two boys must have been with one another every day, and they barely even got along with each other. They would fight all the time: Mo' Money would put a knot on Willie's head, and my son would put one on Mo' Money's, but they would play with one another the very next day. They were the best of friends. The apartment complex where we lived was a fun place for the kids to play, but there were times when it could be dangerous. Willie told me of a frightening incident where he, Mo' Money, and another kid named Kenny had been playing in the stairway when they were approached by two older teenaged boys. The stairways at the apartment were very secluded and not well illuminated. One of the two teenagers pulled out a knife and threatened to cut the kids' penises off if they did not do as they were told. The teenage boys recognized Willie and Mo' Money from hustling in the area, and—thank God!—let them go!

Unfortunately, they kept Kenny as my son and Mo' Money ran home. I don't know for certain what happened to Kenny, but the older boys allegedly sexually assaulted him, and cops were all over the apartment complex that day.

Not too many bad guys came to Mount Zion Apartments and caused trouble thanks to our manager, Mr. Thompson, and our huge maintenance men. However, there was one guy who lived a couple of streets over from the apartments, whose name was Darnell. He was an older teenager and loved to come to the apartments and terrorize the boys with a big knife. The apartments were designed with hallways inside the building. There were stairways at both ends and in the middle of the halls. There were also doors at the stairways. Darnell loved to hide behind those doors and wait for the boys to walk by. Whenever the boys got close to the door, Darnell would jump out from behind it with his big knife. The boys would take off running down the hallway, and Darnell would chase after them. That boy should have been ashamed of himself, scaring those poor kids half to death.

Fortunately, Darnell could never catch the boys. I do not know if he only did it for the excitement, because no one ever got stabbed by Darnell, and you would think that little boys could not outrun him all the time. However, Willie told me of a time when Darnell had been able to corner him, Mo Money, and their friend, Rome. Rome was about three or four years older than Willie and Mo' Money, but he loved to play with them. He enjoyed stirring up fights between the two, and would also pick fights with them and other boys in the area. One day, the three of them were shooting marbles when Darnell slipped up on them. My son said that he does not know how Darnell was able to creep up on them because he had a weird breathing pattern: he made loud grunting noises when he breathed, which was one of the reasons why he had never been able to catch them before. My son said that they could usually hear him breathing from behind the doors, and would take off running in the other direction. However, that day Darnell appeared out of nowhere and yelled, "I got you little muthafuckas now!"

My son said that they almost pissed in their pants when they saw the look on Darnell's face as he clutched his big, shiny knife!

Then Darnell said, "You two Lil' niggas can go! But I'm gonna carve this big punk bitch up!"

My son and Mo' Money took off running full speed down the hallway. Then, all of a sudden, they heard Rome running down the hallway, yelling, "Mama!"

CAPITOL MIDDLE SCHOOL

In 1981, Willie, Mo' Money, and Renae attended Capitol Middle School. This school had more gangs and more fights than did Park Elementary School. Renae, being a year older than Willie, was enrolled at the school first. She was a smart, beautiful girl. Renae would get threatened by girl gangs every day at school. One gang leader told my daughter that they would jump her whenever they saw her. My daughter did not know what to do because there were so many of them.

So I told her to tell the leader of the gang, "You and your gang may beat me every day, but whenever I catch you alone, I will kick your ass, bitch!"

As for Willie, he was already nervous and excited about being in the sixth grade. He was looking forward to leaving elementary school and attending Capitol Middle School. He thought it was a big deal to change classes throughout the day. However, that all changed after he found out that there were other things to be concerned about at the middle school. The older boys at the apartment complex told him and Mo' Money how bad things were going to be at Capitol Middle School. However, once Willie and Mo' Money got to the middle school, they began to fit in with the other hardheaded kids. Somehow, the two of them were in five classes together, but my son and Mo' Money were so bad and disruptive in class that the teachers quickly saw this as a huge problem. The teachers had the boys' schedules redone so that they were no longer allowed to take classes together. After those teachers finished rearranging their schedules, Willie and Mo' Money did not even have lunch at the same time.

Willie began to dress like some of the boys at the school, and even developed a hip walk with a bounce. He loved to come home and imitate how an older guy named Bouncy Dre walked around the school hallways. He wore different-colored pairs of Lee jeans and a variety of patent leather Stacy Adams shoes to school every day. The Stacy Adams shoes were usually black and white, gray and white, or burgundy and white. Bouncy Dre was always clean, and all of his outfits were coordinated from the silk socks to his silk underwear. All of the boys liked to wear their pants sagging with their silk underwear showing. My son said that when Bouncy Dre walked down the hall, it took him about fifteen minutes to go about fifty feet. Bouncy Dre would slam one Stacy Adams shoe to the floor while the other foot was in the air as he bounced to his own beat. He would point both index fingers in the air and say, "Yeah!" as he continued his patented bounce down the school hallway, alternating his feet in a rhythmic motion. Bouncy Dre was rumored to smoke a lot of marijuana, and his eyelids were almost shut. The other students would say, "Bouncy Dre is high as a kite." Unbelievably, the teachers would not say anything to Bouncy Dre when he did his walk. They let him take his sweet time getting to class even though he was often tardy.Everyone got out of the way when he came down the hall. No one fooled with him or dared to step on his Stacy Adam shoes. Bouncy Dre was at least sixteen years old, and should have graduated from middle school and moved on to Capitol High, but had been held back several times. Bouncy Dre was from the Park, but he did not roll with their gang. He was always solo.

The Park and Easy Town were the two major gangs at the school. These gangs were from two huge neighborhoods. There was so much gang activity at the school that security guards had to patrol it during school hours. There were even incidents where the gangs would fight the security officers. The gangs outnumbered the officers, and whenever the gangs fought one another and the officers intervened, the gangs would retaliate against the officers. The gangs were organized according to the neighborhoods where the kids lived. Capitol Middle School was located off Gus Young Avenue in the Park. Therefore, the children from Easy Town had to go through the Park to attend school. The gangs constantly fought one another during and after school. The gangs would go around the school and ask the kids what neighborhood they were from. The gangs would say, "Yeah, you, Mickey Mouse, where you from?" If you were not from their neighborhood, the gangs would then give you a beat down!

This environment influenced my son a lot. He wanted to have all the different-colored Lee jeans, and of course he had to have them starched and sagging off his butt. The jeans had to be cuffed high enough to show the silk socks that matched his shirt. He would also wear matching silk underwear and leather belts. Some of the boys would wear cowhide belts; those were some beautiful belts. They would also have white handkerchiefs in their back pockets and tied around their necks, and wear dark shades. One day, Mo' Money came by the apartment to show my son his brand-new pair of brown suede Hush Puppies; the kids called them "Dawgs." They were a beautiful, expensive pair of shoes. Of course, my son had to have a pair of them, too. I managed to buy him a pair though I was really skeptical about purchasing those shoes. Hush Puppies drew a lot of attention, and kids had even gotten robbed for them. Thankfully, Willie took good care of his shoes, and kept them for a long time. My son never asked for much, especially when it came to shoes and clothes. Even as a little kid, he wore his pants until there were holes in the knees, then got patches and ironed them onto his pants himself; he got a kick out of doing this—he liked how the patches stuck to the material of the pants. However, it was another story when it came to purchasing sneakers. I had to buy him Super Pros tennis shoes for a while. I could not afford the

Converse All Stars that all the boys loved to wear. He wore those Super Pros until he could not stand getting teased at school anymore.

When my son wore those tennis shoes to school, all the other children would laugh and say, "Look at him with those Shit Stompers on!"

However, he never complained about wanting expensive clothes. When it was time to buy school clothes, he was satisfied with the inexpensive t-shirts that I would buy him. I bought the ones that had nice little slogans on them. The t-shirt he loved to wear displayed "MVP" in large letters across the chest, with "most valuable player" spelled out below it. I bought four or five of those t-shirts with three pair of pants, and Willie was good.

CAPITOL HIGH SCHOOL

Willie and Renae told me about an incident that occurred one day while they and Mo' Money were walking home from school. Most of the time, the children had to walk home because I could not afford their city bus fare. During that time, schools did not provide transportation to and from school. Parents had to provide transportation on their own, and the school was over a mile away from where we lived. That day, Mo' Money decided to walk with Willie and Renae even though he had money for the bus, as usual. Walking home from Capitol Middle School, they had to pass Capitol High School. This school was notoriously bad for gang activity, and it was located in Easy Town. As the kids were walking and joking around with one another, a boy suddenly came running from Capitol High School. Two other boys were chasing him, and one of them had a gun. Willie, Renae, and Mo' Money ran as fast as they could away from them, but the boy was heading in their direction. They were terrified as the pursuer started firing the gun at the boy. The children ran at full speed all the way to the apartments. Mount Zion Apartments was bordered with a tall fence, so the children had to run a long way to the front entrance. They ran about fifteen hundred feet from Capitol High School to Mount Zion Apartments, but the children said that it felt like a mile, and that it had felt as though they were running in quicksand because they could not get there fast enough. However, even after they made it to Mount Zion Apartments, the strange boys were heading their way and were very close! The children ran up the stairs to the second floor and hid in a corner within the apartment complex. They watched everything unfold from a window located inside the apartments. The children said that they were sweating, breathing hard, and fearing for their lives. The boy ran into the apartments, still pursued by the shooter and his friend.

Fortunately, he managed to lose the other two boys inside the apartment complex, and made it down the street. That incident was a close call. One of them could have been shot by a stray bullet! It left me worried and terrified about the children having to walk home from school. Before that incident, the children had gotten rides to and from school until Willie and Mo' Money messed it up. The children were commuting with our neighbor, whose daughter attended the same school. However, my son and Mo 'Money teased and harassed the woman's baby, and made him cry every day to and from school. The mother would constantly tell them to stop making her baby boy cry, but they could not resist making boogieman faces at the little baby. Willie and Mo' Money said that the baby had a "funny monkey monk face."

Finally, the mother had enough of Willie and Mo' Money and said, "You two bad asses can find another ride to school!"

However, when the children did have money for the city bus, it was a chaotic ride home. The children informed me of an incident that occurred on the city bus as they left school one day. There was a fight between the two rival gangs, the Park and Easy Town, occurring right across the street from their school. Willie and Mo' Money yelled along with most of the other children on the bus for their neighborhood gang to beat the other one. As the bus left the scene of the fight, the children continued to act out on the bus. Some children were running up and down the aisle, jumping over and across the seats. The bus driver had no control over the bus as the children continued to yell and scream and play. All of a sudden, a loud voice came from a very large, black man with a badge sitting at the back of the bus. He was about six foot four, and muscularly built.

The man said, "I am an undercover cop, and I have been placed on this bus because of complaints about how crazy the children act on this bus route. Everyone on this bus better sit down right now and stop acting like animals before I beat the shit out of you! What in the hell is wrong with you kids? Do you all have any home training? The next kid that acts up on this bus is going to jail."

All of the children who had been misbehaving immediately sat down in their seats, and no one made another sound. You could literally hear a pin drop. The kids had been scared straight! The officer continued to verbally trash the children during the entire bus ride.

Then a young black male interrupted him and said, "Mister, that is enough; the children have stopped misbehaving and there is no need to belittle them anymore."

The officer asked the young man why he had not spoken up when the children had been out of control.

The young black male said, "I do not know why I did not intervene, but it is still no reason for you to continue and talk to the children that way," and exited the bus at the next stop.

CHAPTER 7

THIRTEEN
NEW SURROUNDINGS

MY FIRST HOUSE

After Willie's thirteenth birthday, I purchased my first
home, and we moved from Easy Town to a neighborhood off Scotland Avenue. The kids could not believe
that we had finally moved out of the apartment. The
house was about 1,700 square feet with four bedrooms,
two bathrooms, a living room, an open kitchen, and a
utility room. The utility room was outside, which the
kids hated. They dreaded going out to the utility room

during the winter season. There was an open space behind the house that separated the kitchen from the utility room. You could literally take two steps from the kitchen door and be in the utility room, but the wind could whip so hard through that space that the kids did not want to go out there at all. I guess you could consider it a bad architectural design. We also had a large front and backyard. Willie was responsible for cutting the grass once a week during the summertime. He hated trimming the lawn when the sun was out and beaming, so he got up early on Saturday mornings, before it got too hot. Sometimes his butt would oversleep. Whenever he did that, I would storm into his room and yell for him to get his ass out the bed and cut that damn grass right now! If he didn't move fast enough, I would yank the covers off my son and pull him out the bed by his feet. Making my son cut the grass in the hot sun taught him a lesson about being on time to do your job. I guess that did pay off. To this day, he makes it to work on time.

The kids loved the new house. My daughters had their own bedroom that they did not have to share with their brothers. However, Willie and Monique still fought over the television. Therefore, I made them follow that same old rule: whoever turned it on first in the morning got to watch whatever he or she wanted that day. Those two fighting was reminiscent of the days at the apartment, and at times the kids did miss the old place. We had spent many years there and made unforgettable memories to last a lifetime.

NEW SCHOOL

The kids transferred to their new middle school right after Christmas break. This school's environment was much better: there were a few fights, but no gang activity or security patrol. However, my son would spend most of his time playing in Rockwood, and kept close contact with Mo' Money. They would take turns spending weekends at one another's house. My son faced trouble whenever he went to stay the weekend at Mo' Money's house in Easy Town, because Mo' Money had started hanging out with the gangs in the area. There was one guy who had never gotten along with my son when we had lived there. He tried to stir up mess among the other gang members and Willie.

He would tell my son, "Hey, Willie Gat, you moved to the other side of town, and we don't fuck with them niggas from there, you heard me."

But Mo' Money would get them to back off and say, "Man, y'all know Willie Gat go way back with us, so stop trippin', fools!"

My son was playing football and basketball at his new school, and doing quite well. This was his first time playing organized sports with a team. He and Mike Black remained very close and attended school together. They were both heavily involved in sports, and played football and basketball from sunup to sundown. I would have to threaten my son with the belt if he did not make it home before the streetlights came on. Whenever he did not, I met him at the door with the belt, and beat his butt all the way to his bedroom.

I think my son began to be interested in girls at around this age, though he did not speak to any. He had a crush on the prettiest girls at his school and would ask his sister, Renae, for advice on what to say to them on the phone. Renae told him to write some questions on a sheet of paper before he called them. She told her brother to ask them questions like, "When is your birthday?" and "What is your sign?" But even after Willie built up the nerve to call these girls and engage them in conversation, they did not respond well to Willie or give any vibes that they liked him. So my son never called them again.

I must say...

I was very proud of my son for learning how to cut his own hair at a young age. "Big O," an older boy he befriended in middle school, taught him how to do it. That was really a lifelong lesson that saved my son plenty of money over the years. One of my son's best traits is the ability to save money—Willie is one tight son of a gun. He cuts his own hair to this day.

My family struggled financially until my kids were teenagers and got jobs of their own. They were pretty much able to take care of themselves after that. They were some very independent kids who had to grow up fast.

CHAPTER 8

FOURTEEN
PEER PRESSURE

HOOD MARKS

When Willie turned fourteen, peer pressure started to have an impact on him. He finally managed to convince me to buy him the gold tooth that I disapproved of. He had always wanted a gold tooth and diamond earring just like his father's. A lot of his friends were getting gold teeth, and he had to have one, too. Unfortunately, he had chipped his tooth playing football when he was young, and the caps and crowns the dentist had used all came off or changed colors. Eventually, I got tired of taking him back and forth to and from the dentist, and therefore gave in to that gold tooth. It cost $400 and you could see it shining from a mile away. He also had his friend from Rockwood, "Bay Bay," tattoo him against my instruction. I had told him that I was not about to have him looking like a little thug, so he tried to have the tattoos placed someplace where I would not notice. He had his friend ink his legs, figuring that his pants would hide the tattoos from me.

The tattoos that his friend gave him were not done in a method used in the certified tattoo industry. These tattoos are known as "jailhouse tattoos," and are done using a bottle of black India ink and a needle. The ink is drawn on your body first, then the needle repeatedly sticks the drawing until it punches the pattern into your skin. Sometimes the person doing the tattooing will stick your body first until your pattern is formed in blood; then the ink is placed over the bloody pattern until it sinks into the skin. This method of tattooing is very unsafe! However, Willie and his friends all got tattoos with their nicknames, initials, or gang pictures on their bodies. I had forbidden him from ever getting tattoos, but he went against my wishes and placed his initials on his legs. My youngest daughter, Monique, spotted them, and though Willie pleaded with her not say anything, she revealed them to me. But by that time I had retired from whipping him with the belt; he was just too big, and I was tired of beating him by now.

STEALING BICYCLES

Some of Willie's friends stole things. My father and I had raised my son to never steal, and he knew that I would "break his neck!" if he ever did. We had taught him to work for the things he wanted in life, and that if he did not have the money for something, it was better to go without. My son bought a beautiful burgundy and white Cruiser bicycle with the money he had made working with Drew. The kids called them "hogs" or "trucks." The bike had those thick, pretty, white wall tires and wide, chrome handlebars and fenders; he loved to go and buy reflectors, shingles, and mirrors for it. However, the friends he hung out with did not think twice about stealing. They would all get on their bicycles, and the ones who did not have bikes of their own would ride on the handlebars of their friends' bikes. Then they would ride off to other neighborhoods several miles away, and when they returned to Rockwood, all of them would have bicycles. They all would gather around and joke about how funny, scared, and nervous their friend looked stealing a bike. They would reenact the entire scene, especially the part when the person was pedaling away on the bike and the entire bike shook from side to side because their friend had been so scared that he was unable to place his feet on the pedals. They all thought that was so funny. They would choose bikes that had been left outside and unsecured. This is also the time that he began to drink alcohol with his homeboys. He and his friends would get an older guy from the neighborhood to purchase a forty-ounce bottle of beer for five or six of them to share. Over a period of time, one forty-ounce bottle was not enough for them all. So they started buying their own individual forty-ounce bottles of beer.

THE BIRDS AND THE BEES

The time my son was going through puberty had to be when he became sexually active. However, I had started to wonder when he would show an interest in girls instead of hanging with his homeboys all the time. So I spoke with Big Unc concerning Willie dating girls.

He told me, "Daula, don't worry, Willie will show interest in them real soon—and when he does, look out! Girls will be on his mind twenty-four/seven. You just better pray he does not get anyone pregnant."

Oh my goodness, that made me think of his father. Dumplin had kids all over the place! My children had half-brothers and half-sisters they had never seen or even heard of before; I had been told as much by Dumplin's closest friend. I knew that he had a set of twin girls and little boy, but I did not know of any other kids. That was something I did not want for my son. I had to make sure that my child did not have illegitimate children all over the place like his father. I was going to raise him to not have kids until he got married. More so, to be a man and take care of the children he did have. I did not know how to speak to my son about the birds and the bees, so I simply gave him a condom.

I told him, "Boy, you better use this condom if you decide to have sex. You know how much I struggled raising y'all, and furthermore, there are too many diseases out there that you could catch and you will not be able to get rid of!"

He seemed very uncomfortable when I gave the condom to him. He kept his head down the entire time and didn't look up until I left. I know this was tough for him to hear from me. I think it would have been much better coming from a man who could discuss this with him. I did not want him to have kids at an early age like I had done. I noticed that he placed the condom in his wallet. I think I must have checked his wallet once a week when he was asleep to see if that boy had used the condom.

Just as I began to wonder if he was even having sex, my sister, Belle, called me from Rockwood and said, "Daula, I heard that Willie, Bay Bay, Roe, Lil' Boonie, and Mike Black ran a train on a girl from the neighborhood. They all took turns having sex with her!"

I could not believe my ears. All I could think was, *Dang, I hope he used that condom.*

Willie never knew it, but I checked his wallet when he went to sleep the night that Belle called. I had to see if the condom was still in his wallet.

Oh my goodness… it was not!

He must have listened to me and used the condom that I had given him. If that condom had been left in his wallet while he'd had unprotected sex, I think I would have lost my mind on my son that night. I would have been so disappointed and upset. I really would not have known what else to tell him. I was not happy about him having sex, but I was relieved that he had listened to me and used the condom.

❖ ❖ ❖

I think most people know of at least one girl in their neighborhood that "all the boys have been with." You know, the one who is "loose in the caboose."

Most neighborhoods have at least one promiscuous girl in it, but this girl did not fit the description at all. Her name was Joanna. She was a quiet girl, and a straight-A student in high school. She was very pretty with long, beautiful, black hair; a light complexion; and a slender body frame with a huge chest. If you did not know the gossip, you would not suspect Joanna of ever doing such a thing. Most of the girls in Rockwood did not like Joanna and did not want her around their boyfriends.

People would say that whenever the neighborhood boys saw her taking an evening walk with one of her girlfriends, they would call her over to talk, and the next thing you knew, she would be inside the house having sex with all of them. I think my son spent a lot of time with Joanna, because he was always chilling on the street near her house.

Big Unc was right about my son and girls. I later found out that that sneaky joker was having sex with his sister's girlfriends whenever they slept over at our house on the weekends. I just prayed that he always used condoms. His younger cousin, Hoss, had already gotten a girl pregnant, and he was only thirteen!

CHAPTER 9

FIFTEEN
JUVENILE BEHAVIOR

MARIJUANA

This was the time when a lot of my son's troubles began. After Willie failed to make the varsity high school football and basketball teams, his desire to become a professional athlete was over. My son was the type of person who wanted to win at everything he did. Becoming a professional athlete is most young men's dream, but achieving it is a highly unlikely feat that is not accomplished with talent alone. You need to have a lot of other factors go your way, and to have good timing. Even if you are more talented than a person who makes it to the professional level, one bad decision or coach can go against your favor. Some teenage boys engage in trouble after they stop playing high school sports. They tend to start running with the neighborhood gangs, and get involved with drugs and alcohol. I noticed that my son began to pack knives around this time. He had two knives: a switchblade and a lock-blade. He began smoking marijuana often during this period. I remember telling him not to smoke marijuana because it would lead him to use heavier drugs, like cocaine. One summer afternoon, Willie's childhood friend, Mo' Money, came to visit my son and show off his new car: it was a burgundy 1977 Grand Prix. Mo' Money had converted it into a low rider, and had put those expensive chrome Truespoke wire wheel rims on it. My son could not wait to get a car of his own after seeing Mo' Money's ride.

JACKING CAR STEREOS

Jeana is my youngest sister, and her husband, Devin, got Willie his first job as a busboy at a five-star Italian restaurant where the food was authentic and delicious;

the owners of the restaurant were originally from Italy, and the menu displayed that distinction. Willie was able to afford a car at the age of fifteen with the money he earned at the restaurant. This was a great job for him: it provided him with good tips, responsibilities, and experience with budgeting money. Along with the car came our first encounter with the police. Willie was arrested on the Louisiana State University (LSU) campus along with some other boys for breaking into cars and stealing their stereos. Willie said that the cops were trying to get them all to snitch on one another. They even showed my son written statements in which the other boys stated that Willie had been the one who had broken into the cars, not them. The police asked Willie if he wanted to write a statement concerning the other boys breaking into the cars. My son told the officers that he had not broken into any cars, and that he did not want to write a statement about anyone else. Willie was later released. The police determined that Willie was not the one who had broken into the cars and stolen the stereos. Willie later explained to me that he had only gone along for the ride to get first choice on purchasing the stereos from his homeboy from Rockwood. He eventually realized how stupid this decision was, and purchased his own car stereo with money he earned working at the restaurant.

WILLIE'S FIRST CAR

I should have paid more attention to my son wanting high-quality audio for his car. I had just bought a brand-new 1986 Buick Regal Limited, and Willie had the nerve to take the speakers out of my car and replace them with his old car speakers. He said that my car speakers sounded better and carried more bass. His car was a 1981 Chevy Monte Carlo that he had bought before he was old enough to possess a driver's license. That car was his pride and joy. As the kids would say, he "pimped it out" with a sound system, tinted windows, chrome spoke rims, and two-inch white wall tires. He and his friend, Roe, from Rockwood "dropped it" and made it into a low rider.

Willie loved to say, "I got the cleanest Monte Carlo in the BR. You heard me!"

Another one of his sayings for girls who rode in his car was, "In order to ride, you must ride!"

I remember the time when my son had to pick me up from school because my car was in the shop. I was so embarrassed to ride in that car. And to make matters worse, my coworkers were getting off from work and saw me drive away in that car. We did not get a mile down the road before a cop pulled us over. The cop said that he had pulled my son over because his windows were tinted too dark. The cop told Willie that the next time he saw him cruising down the highway, the dark tint had better be out of his windows. Oh, Willie had a fit! He said that removing the dark tint from his windows would change the entire look of his car. I told him that he did not have a choice; that cop meant business, and would definitely be on the lookout for his car. I was so glad to get out of that low rider. I did understand how my son drove with all the hopping and bouncing that car did. It literally danced down the roadway. I warned my son not to put all that stuff on his car, because one day, someone would steal it.

HIS FIRST GIRLFRIEND

My son shocked me when he brought his first girlfriend, Wanda, home for me to meet one Christmas. It was funny how they had met: someone had set up a blind date between my son and Wanda's sister. My son and my nephew, Mike Black, met the two girls at the movies. My son said that when he saw Wanda, he could not take his eyes off her. Wanda's sister was totally not his type, and she was more into Mike Black. Well, everyone figured out what was going on, so the two couples switched dates, and Wanda and my son became a couple. Word got back to me that his little mannish butt was having that girl skip school to have sex with him at my house while everyone was gone. I wanted to wring his neck for that. I thought he was not interested in having a steady girlfriend. I think this was the first time that he fell in love with a girl. My son said that they dated off and on for a couple of years, and that he even bought her a diamond ring with the tip money he earned as a busboy. I never asked him why they broke up, but I think they always remained friends.

COCAINE

It was 1985, and cocaine was the hottest drug on the streets. Mo' Money was heavily involved in the game, and making a lot of cash. My son would go visit Mo' Money at his house in Easy Town, and there would be stacks of tens, twenties, fifties, and hundred-dollar bills all over the bedroom floor. Mo' Money had been expelled from Capitol High School for dealing drugs. Willie said that Mo' Money had all the latest sneakers, clothes, jewelry, cars, girls, and of course, cash money. My son said that there were at least twenty boxes of brand-new Fila and Nike tennis shoes along the wall in Mo' Money's bedroom. Mo' Money had bought a Z-28 Camaro, two Cadillacs, and a 1966 Chevrolet Impala. He placed Truespokes and Vogue tires on them, and pimped out the cars' interiors with customized diamond seat designs. That Camaro had the loudest music my son said he had ever heard before: it had five Punch 18" woofers with two Punch amps in it, and it sounded like a volcano had erupted when Mo' Money cranked it up! Mo' Money had even changed his front teeth to gold, and had placed diamonds in them. As the kids would say, Mo' Money was "rolling hard." He was breaking bread with the major players of gangs and hoods in "the BR!" My son said that Mo' Money was getting with the Park, Easy Town, Banks Town, Rockwood, Fairfield, Belfair, Mall City, Zion City Smurfs, South Side Wrecking Crew, and many others.

❖ ❖ ❖

I constantly told my son not to get involved with that life, that it was a dead-end future. This was very hard for my son to realize. The longer Mo' Money sold cocaine without getting busted, the more Willie wanted to get in the game. He began to frequent Easy Town, the old neighborhood we had moved away from, and hung out more often with Mo' Money.

My son discussed his first experience with cocaine with me. He was at Mo' Money's house, and there was an empty plastic bag with cocaine residue in it.

My son asked Mo' Money, "Man, why are people so crazy about that stuff?"

Mo Money told Willie, "Chew on a small piece of that empty bag and see what's up."

My son looked at Mo' Money like he was crazy.

Mo' Money said, "It ain't gon' do nothing to you, man." Then Mo' Money tore a piece of the bag, placed it in his mouth, and chewed it.

My son said that his curiosity got the best of him that day, and he also put a piece of the bag into his mouth. Willie said that his entire mouth and throat immediately went numb, and sensational thoughts rushed through his head!

CHAPTER 10

SIXTEEN
GOT IN THE GAME

GOT IN THE GAME

At this age, Willie began to smoke marijuana regularly, and was not doing well in school. My sister, Belle, told me that she would see Willie and a group of his friends smoking marijuana on the corner in Rockwood. This is the time when everything began to go downhill for my son. He was bored with high school and did not want to be there, and though he was never held back a grade, he was only doing just enough to get by. Whenever he and his homeboys met to discuss and show off their grades, his friends had all Ds and Fs on their report cards, and Willie would tell them that his grades were bad, too. However, after he showed them report cards that consisted of mostly Cs and a couple of Ds, they all laughed at him and declared that they would take Willie Gat's grades any day. My son had good relationships with some of his teachers, but really bad ones with others. One of his teachers told him that he would not be successful in life, and would end up in jail. She wanted to give him a failing grade in her class even after he passed the final examination, despite her policy of advancing every student who passed the final exam. She did not like the fact that my son had done nothing in her class all year besides making smart comments that made the other students laugh. For him to pass her final exam and proceed to the next class was not acceptable to her. I had to meet with her over this issue, and reiterate to her what the policy clearly stated. I explained that my son had met his obligations. Therefore, she had no choice, but to advance him to the next class. During this time, my son started spending a lot more time with Mo' Money. I thought nothing of it because they had kept in touch since we'd moved away from Easy Town. However, by this time, Mo' Money had gotten real big in the game. It was rumored on the streets that he made a million dollars from dealing cocaine before he turned eighteen. Mo' Money was also infatuated with high-powered weapons. He kept all kinds of semiautomatic weapons with banana clips in his possession. His favorite was the AK-47, and he enjoyed showing it off to my son.

DEVIN

In the fall of September 1987, my son witnessed a horrible event: he saw Devin get shot and killed. His shooting occurred one night after business hours at the Italian restaurant where Willie and Devin worked. The majority of the employees who worked there was black, and employed as waiters, valets, cooks, bartenders, and dishwashers. On Sunday nights, the employees usually had a few drinks before they got off work. My son said that a few drinks usually lead to a lot of drinks, and Devin was having his usual share of them on that night.

There was another waiter named Stuart with whom Devin constantly joked around. They would crack on one another all the time, and regularly pop each other with their towels. All of the waiters and even the maître d' joked around with one another at work, all day, every day. My son said that it felt like going to a live comedy show. There was this one quiet, female, middle-aged dishwasher who was a very heavy drinker. My son said that that lady's body was well put-together: it resembled the shape of a Coke bottle. Her name was Ms. Ree.

My son said that for some reason that night, Devin was "in a zone:" he was ragging on Stuart hard that day, and it continued in the parking lot. Stuart was supposed to give Ms. Ree a ride home from work. Devin was still riding Stuart's ass, cracking on him all the way to his car. Devin was carpooling home with my son that night, and my boy got his car and drove over to pick up Devin. My son pulled up right beside Stuart's car on the passenger side, where Ms. Ree was sitting. Devin was over by the driver's side, still fooling around with Stuart.

Then Stuart produced a gun from his car and said, "Okay, Devin, your ass better leave now. You see I got my .357 Magnum with me!"

Devin replied, "Stuart, your bitch ass ain't gon' do nothing with that gun, fool!"

Stuart laughed and put the gun down.

Eerily, Ms. Ree picked up the gun and started waving it around as she sat in the front seat of Stuart's car, her head rolling around and around.

Devin left Stuart, went over to Ms. Ree's side of the vehicle, and said, "Okay, Ms. Ree, you got the gun. Now what are you gonna do with it?"

Ms. Ree responded drunkenly, "I—I'll shoot you—me!"

A strange calmness appeared in the air, and everything went silent until there was a loud *pow!*

Then Devin said, "Oh no, Ms. Ree, you shot me!" Then he fell back to the ground.

Ms. Ree sat back in the car seat like a zombie!

Stuart came running around the car yelling, "Oh shit, what the fuck! Oh shit, what the fuck!"

The restaurant owner lived on the property, so my son ran to her house as fast as he could and told her to call an ambulance because Devin had just been shot. However, when my son looked around, Stuart had already left with Devin en route to the hospital. Later that night, all of our family gathered at the hospital, hoping and praying that Devin would be okay. Unfortunately, he did not make it!

This was a devastating experience for Willie because he and Devin had spent a lot of time together, and had been very close. My sister's husband was like a big brother to my son. Devin had grown up a single child, and had had quite a privileged life. His parents bought him a brand new sports car when he was a young teen, and he had a brick house waiting for him whenever he got married. His sports car was his pride and joy, and he enjoyed blasting his music and racing other Z-28 Camaros. Devin was also a courageous guy: he never backed down, and would fight anyone.

My son told me about the time some guys in Devin's new neighborhood, the Lakes, wanted to gang him. Devin had moved out of Rockwood but still hung out there. So he rounded up some of his homeboys from Rockwood and met the guys from the Lakes at a high school football game. Devin said that the fight went down after the football game, and that the boys from the Lakes got hurt.

Devin loved to kid around and have a good time. He and Willie horsed around all day, every day. He and Jeana had been childhood sweethearts, and everyone knew that the two of them would get married. They were a perfect match. Willie was even in their wedding. And when it came to drinking, Devin could drink anyone under the table without getting drunk. He was actually the first person who introduced alcohol to my son. Willie would constantly ask Devin to buy him beer, but Devin would tell Willie that he was not ready for beer yet, and bought him a wine cooler instead.

Devin got my son his first real job. They commuted to work together every day until Willie bought his own car, an '81 Chevrolet Monte Carlo. This tragedy was tough on the entire family, and hard to believe. Devin and Jeana had had a little girl named Shalon, and Jeana was pregnant with a second child, Kashly, at the time of the horrible incident. Devin was only twenty-one years old at the time of his death.

Ms. Ree was not charged with anything. The court decided that Devin's death had been an accident.

JEANA'S HOUSE

When I met my husband, Burt, Willie was sixteen and not receptive to having a new man in his life. He and Burt argued constantly. Sometimes, Willie would come home drunk, and challenge Burt to tell him what he could and could not do. Willie would have girls in his room when no one was home, though Burt had told him not to be locked away in his room with girls.

I cannot for the life of me forget about the time Renae and I were sitting in the room, talking, and her son, Boogie, walked into the room. Boogie was about seven years old then. He was wearing his uncle Willie's gold chain and diamond cross around his neck. He also had on Willie's sneakers, and had hundred-dollar bills in both fists and hanging out of his front and back pockets. I immediately got up and barged into Willie's room. Shockingly, I saw cash money everywhere! There were thousands of dollars tied in rubber bands all over his bed and on the floor.

I asked my son, "What the hell is going on!"

He replied, "Ma, why you trippin', coming into my room like that!"

I told him, "This is my damn house and I demand to know what the hell is going on!" Then I said, "Willie, is this dope money?"

He looked at me like I was crazy, and said, "Ma, I am just handling my business!"

I told that little asshole, "I will not have drug activity going on under my roof, and if you are going to continue down that road, get the hell out of my house!"

Disappointingly, my son chose to take the dope-dealing route and moved out of the house to live in Rockwood with my youngest sister, Jeana, following the loss of her husband.

My son and Jeana were three years apart and had grown up together. Jeana was more like a sister to my kids than an aunt. She would spend the weekends at my apartment in Easy Town all the time. My son had a lot of freedom living with Jeana, and did pretty much whatever he wanted at her house. You could really say that he had a blast living with his aunt. Her house was located one street over and directly behind Joanna's house. That boy of mine would call Joanna on the phone to come over and have sex with him when his aunt was not home. It was really easy for Joanna to walk out of her house and jump the fence in Jeana's backyard. By this time, Joanna had stopped having sex with all the homeboys in the neighborhood, and would only have sex with Willie.

MOLLY

Eventually, Willie got a steady girlfriend named Molly. Molly was one year older than my son, but that did not bother him. He really liked Molly, and the two of them got along great. She could do hair, and always kept herself looking nice. The two of them met one day after a concert at the downtown Centroplex. Willie was driving around the area in his car with Mike Black and Roe. Molly said that Willie pulled up beside her girlfriend's car and got her attention. He then told them to pull over so he could "holla at me." Molly recalled the meeting very well.

She said, "It was crazy...Mike Black and Roe jumped into our car and started talking to my two girlfriends, and Willie Gat was trying to get me to leave with him." She went on to say that you could tell that all of them had been drinking. Molly said that there was no way she was going anywhere with Willie that day, but could not resist from giving him her number because he was so cute and funny.

Willie said, "Hey, Molly how about you roll with me, and my homeboys can roll with your homegirls."

Molly laughed and said, "And where are we going, Willie Gat?"

Then Willie said, "Get naked!"

Molly burst out laughing and told Willie that he was crazy.

My son then told Molly that he was playing and just wanted to hang out with her. Molly told Willie that she had to get home to her baby, but maybe they could go to the movies or something next weekend. Molly had a little baby boy whom everyone adored. They did end up going to the movies the next weekend, and spent a lot of time together. Molly visited Willie just about every weekend at Jeana's house, and usually spent the night there. He brought Molly home to meet his family. Willie and Molly dated for quite some time, and my son met her mom and family as well. Molly had been friends with my daughter, Renae, at Capitol Middle School. My son said that he remembered Molly from back then, but she did not remember him. I think this was the second time he fell in love with a girl. I never asked him why they broke up, but I think they always remained friends.

DEEPER IN THE GAME

While at Jeana's house, my son was getting into one thing after another, and had gotten deeper into the game.

He was hanging out on the street corner all night, hustling hard in Rockwood. After a year or so, I made him come back home, though he continued to be discontent with my husband. I remember the time when I had just lost my home due to ballooning interest rates. My son approached me while I was cooking dinner; I had just finished stirring the cornbread mix and placed the empty box on the counter. I was still very upset from losing my house, and had barely finished unpacking things in the duplex where I did not want to be.

My son walked into the kitchen and said to me, "How do you lose your house after you get married?"

I grabbed the cornbread box and smacked him in his face with it!

He stared at me for about a minute with a frown all over his face, said, "You better be glad you're my mama!" and walked away.

However, when my son became an adult, he and Burt became really good friends. They went fishing together and talked sports and politics for hours at a time. Sometimes, Willie called Burt to get advice on vehicle repairs and business decisions. Their relationship is really good now!

CHAPTER 11

SEVENTEEN
IN IT

SERIOUS TROUBLE

1988 was Willie's senior year in high school, and this was when serious trouble began. To start things off, I found a pistol in his book bag.

I asked my son, "Boy, why the hell do you have a gun in your book bag?"

He said, "Them fools at school trippin'; somebody tried to hotwire my car!"

I asked him, "Did you report it to your school?

He said, "No, "I'm gon' handle it!"

I told that boy that he was losing his damn mind, and I had my brother, LC, take the pistol from him.

By this time, my son was ready to finish high school and had mentioned to me that he found it to be really boring. He was tired of school, and did not to want to attend college. So he challenged himself to load up on extra classes and graduate early. None of his friends and teachers thought that he could do it, because he had never pushed himself in school, and had only done enough to get by. That year, my son worked as hard as he had ever worked in school before to prove everyone wrong and accomplish his goal.

Willie did it! He passed all the necessary classes and graduated a semester early. It showed him that he could do whatever he wanted if he pushed himself, and that actually made my son consider going to college. I still cannot believe all that hard work he put in. My son did not go back to the high school and march with his class in the commencement ceremony. That boy of mine had the school mail him his diploma.

CAR STOLEN

Well, he was out of high school and had not enrolled in college yet. He was just having himself a ball, running the streets all night and hanging on the street corner. He was staying out late at night and sleeping in every morning. One morning, he woke up with a terrible hangover. However, that was not the worst of it.

That morning, his aunt Jeana approached him and said, "Willie, where is your car?"

My son said that he looked on the dresser and saw that his car keys were still there. He walked over to the bedroom window and looked outside, but he did not see his car in the driveway. Then he stumbled through the house and walked out the front door to make sure his eyes were not deceiving him. Unfortunately, they were not—his car was gone.

My son grabbed his head with both of his hands and said, "Damn, them hoes got me!"

Word quickly got around the neighborhood that someone had stolen Willie Gat's car. My son and some of his homeboys drove around to neighborhoods that were known for selling items from stolen cars, but had no luck. A few weeks later, the cops called and told us that they had found my son's car. It had been stripped of the tires and rims, and the sound system had been taken from it. The police told us that we could come and pick the vehicle up from their yard. My son told them to keep the car. That incident left him very upset!

RENAE'S WEDDING

The summer of 1997 was a beautiful season. My oldest daughter, Renae, married her high school sweetheart, and we had a fabulous reception in the backyard of my house. A lot of people attended the event, including my co-workers, family, and friends. My husband and I rented a big, beautiful tent for the wedding. Everything was decorated very nicely with flowers and ornaments. There was plenty of food and drink. Everyone was singing, dancing, and having a marvelous time. Later that evening, as things were winding down, Willie had too much to drink and started to act a fool! No one could calm him down. My husband, Burt, tried to get him to chill out, and they began to argue. Apparently, my son was still upset about a fight he'd had with some guys from the neighborhood. Finally, his aunt Jeana managed to get him inside the house. She was known to calm

Willie down whenever he'd had too much to drink and got out of control.

It was hard to believe that beer was enough to make Willie act a damn fool!

Then out of nowhere, he yelled,

"I wanna fuck Molly!

"Go get Molly!"

"Go get Molly!"

Molly had left the wedding early because she had no babysitter that evening. I remember Renae calling Molly and telling her that Willie was drunk and wanted her to come over, now! Renae told her that we would babysit if she came over to see her brother. Molly agreed, and we went and picked her up.

She and my son dated for quite some time, and we all thought that they would get married. However, when Willie started college, their relationship changed, and they eventually broke up.

IN TOO DEEP

However, before enrolling in college, my son had other things on his mind. Mike Black and Ro got in the game and sold drugs with Willie at the same time. Sadly, Mike

Black and Ro started using cocaine and got addicted to it. They shot the cocaine into their veins instead of selling it. Willie broke ties with them as far as selling drugs was concerned, and continued to get himself deeper into the game. I found rolls of cash in his pants pockets whenever I washed his clothes, and I did not think that he earned those kinds of tips working at the restaurant as a busboy. There were desperate times when I needed a little bit of money for gas, and the cash I would find in his pants pockets did come in handy. Shamefully, I actually began to enjoy washing his pants because he usually left money in them. Around this time, my son began to drink more, and stayed out in the streets all night. I could not understand how he was able to function after drinking all day and night until my sister, Belle, told me that she overheard Willie, Mike Black, and Ro one weekend in her outdoor laundry room.

They were snorting cocaine, and Willie said, "Man, if I had too much to drink, I could take two bumps and I was straight, you heard me." They considered "a bump" to mean an amount of cocaine about the size of a fingertip.

He made it home that night at around 2:00 in the morning and sat in the living room to watch television.

I approached him and said, "Boy, it's really late. Why are you up watching T.V.?"

He replied, "Because I am not sleepy."

I then said, "Are you doing cocaine? You know your daddy is strung out on that shit! Is that who you want to be like in life? Boy, I raised you better than that!"

My son replied, "Ma, ain't nobody hooked on dope! You trippin'!"

He then made a phone call and left the house.

There was not one night that I got a good night's sleep while he was out there in those streets. Whenever I heard his music playing as he pulled in the driveway, I would hop out of bed and meet him at the door. I always said to him, "Boy, you made it home," and he would mumble something so as to appear upset with me for checking up on him.

Every night, I went to bed afraid to hear the phone ring. I did not want to get a disturbing phone call about my son. I did not want to believe that Willie was selling cocaine. He was still working at the restaurant, and had started attending college. He had gotten another restaurant job at a private country club after the theft of his car and the death of Devin. Willie hated going to that job. Shortly before my son turned eighteen, he bought a powder white Jeep and spent a lot of money installing a booming sound system in it. He put in those enormous eighteen-inch woofer speakers with a powerful amplifier. You could literally hear him coming from a mile away. He loved to play Gigolo Tony's album, *Ice Cold*. However, the song that he played all the time was by the rapper Slick Rick. It was titled, "Children's Story." Willie loved to enter the neighborhood where he hung out bumping that song. People knew that he was in the neighborhood whenever they heard it. I must admit, it was also my favorite song to hear him play. Willie kept cash and wore nice clothes and jewelry. I did tell him not to keep all that loud music in his Jeep because someone would steal it, and sure enough, someone broke into his Jeep while he was at work and stole his sound system. He was very angry about it, but turned right back around and replaced the entire system in his Jeep the very next day.

CHANTAL'S PROM NIGHT

Willies next encounter with the police involved getting his tail out of jail for aggravated assault, damaging private property, and disturbing the peace. Willie, Mike Black, Roe, and Roy had been drinking beer all day, and trouble usually followed a large amount of alcohol consumption. They had switched to light beer, but increased the volume that they drank. They were all intoxicated when they had a confrontation in Rockwood with some other guys from another neighborhood.

That night, someone must have called the cops and given them my son's name, description, and the make and model of his car, because the police pulled him over as he was heading down the highway. Willie had a girl with him, and police took them both to the jail. The young lady he had with him was named Chantal. She was from Rockwood, and was madly in love with Willie. It was no secret how Chantal felt about him. All the girls in the area knew that Chantal was crazy about Willie, because she let them know as much if they ever got involved with him.

Embarrassingly, Chantal was arrested on her prom night while fooling around with my son! Initially, she had spoken with him about him taking her to prom, but Willie told her, "I don't fuck with prom, but we can hook up afterwards. You heard me."

Later that night, when Chantal was talking to her prom date at her house, Willie drove up with his music thumping and told Chantal to get in his Jeep. Chantal got into the Jeep and left her date standing there. I remembered having to go to the police station and take Chantal home in her beautiful prom dress. I apologized to her for my son's actions and told Chantal to never go anywhere with Willie if he had been drinking! The charges for aggravated assault, damaging property, and disturbing the peace were later dismissed, but my son had to pay a fine.

During this period in his life, my son was drinking every day and hustling on the street corner at night, but still managed to keep a job and attend college.

GANG FIGHT

There was another incident that involved a fight with him and the gang from our new neighborhood. He had been partying and drinking all day, and had a confrontation with a gang member. Some of the gang member's homeboys jumped in and beat Willie down. My son was beaten very badly. He had knots on his head, swollen jaws, bruised ribs, and a chipped tooth. Willie was furious about the ordeal! Immediately after the fight, he returned to the scene to get the guys who had ganged him. It seemed as though nothing could stop him; he looked as though he were possessed.

My brother, LC, tried to stop him from going back to get those guys because Willie was in no condition to fight. However, nothing anyone said or did could calm him down.

LC took out his gun and put it to my son's head, then asked him if he wanted to die!

My son replied, "You got the gun, what are you going to do with it?" and LC was speechless.

Willie then did something unbelievable: he slapped LC's hand while his finger was still on the trigger with the gun pointing to my son's head. Fortunately, the gun did not go off, and LC walked away, shaking his head in disbelieve.

My son immediately took off running to the neighborhood to find the guys who had ganged him. Willie was walking down the street in their neighborhood with his hands in the air, yelling for those boys to come out! He even went to one boy's house looking for him. However, no one came out of the house, and he did not find the others.

Shortly after that happened, a guy robbed my son at gunpoint for drugs and money. However, none of these incidents persuaded him to get out the game!

CHAPTER 12

EIGHTEEN
THE SHOOTING

CONFRONTATION

It was the summer of August 1989 when I received the phone call that I so desperately had not wanted to get. I had spoken to my son earlier that day and told him not to hang out in the streets; I had a bad feeling about that night. He had just gotten out of jail for aggravated assault, disturbing the peace, and damaging private property. Nonetheless, he was eager to get back on the street corner.

I recall my brother, LC, telling me, "Your son, Willie Gat, has the entire hood sewed up." "No one else hustles in Rockwood."

Besides, one bad incident after another had occurred that week. It was around 1:00 a.m. when the phone rang.

It was my mother who said, "Daula, Willie has shot and killed someone!" I frantically asked my mother, "Where is he?

"And what happen?"

She said to me, "Willie had a confrontation with three gang members at a house party in your old neighborhood off Scotland Avenue." "One gang member was shot and killed, another one was shot and injured, and the third guy was not hit!' "Willie is at my house right now, and we are trying to get him to calm down. He has been yelling up a storm!" "He is very angry and upset!" "Daula, you need to come right away!"

After hearing that troubling news, I immediately jumped out the bed with my heart pounding, and rushed to my mother's house. For the first time in my life, I was mad, nervous, and scared all at the same time. I was literally sick to my stomach and did not know what to do.

Mama had helped me raise my son. She would always talk to my boy and tell him positive things to do. She was the grandmother that all the grandchildren loved and adored. She always talked to Willie and he listened to her.

Once I reached my son, I did not know if I should have choked or hugged him. Nevertheless, he immediately explained to me what happened.

My son said that three gang members had approached him and Mike Black, and one of them had a gun drawn. Sadly, my son and Mike Black knew the gang members, and were even cool with the one who was killed; they had all been friends in middle school. However, my son said that they still quarreled with him over some girl he knew nothing about.

My son told them, "Look, brah, I don't know what fuckin' girl y'all talking about, and don't come at me with no dumb shit!"

The gang member with the gun in his hand said, "Fuck you, Willie Gat, ol' bitch-ass, pussy-ass nigga...You know what girl we talking about, ho!"

Willie replied, "Fuck you, ol' ho-ass nigga!"

My son told me that Mike Black tried to squash the confrontation, but the gang members did not listen to anything he said, and the feud escalated! They all kept going back and forth, cursing at one another.

My son said again, "Man, how the fuck y'all gon' come at me about some bitch! You ho-ass niggas better get the fuck out my face with dat bullshit, you heard me!"

The gang member with the gun said, "Naw, bitch, you fuckin' with my homeboy's girl, and you gon' get dealt with!"

My son told me that his life was threatened, and he had to protect himself. So, he got the .44 Magnum out of his Jeep and handled his business!

After I heard that, I told him to turn himself in to the police, and that we would get everything cleared. I asked my brother, LC, to accompany us to the police station, and we followed Willie in his vehicle.

Cops were everywhere with their lights and sirens blasting as we drove to the police station. They got behind Willie's vehicle and demanded that he pull over. They had him place his hands out the window and exit his vehicle slowly. The officers approached him with their guns drawn. They searched my son up and down.

ARRESTED

They handcuffed Willie and put him in a police car. They thoroughly searched his vehicle but did not find anything. They then had his vehicle impounded, and drove Willie to the police station. My brother and I were parked a few cars down from the police cars and witnessed everything. My son told me that they kept him up all night, asking him questions. He cooperated with the detectives at the police station, answering all of their questions and telling them everything that happened that night. Even though Willie spoke with the detectives, this is something that I highly recommend against doing without legal representation. My son should have not spoken to them without an attorney present. He was facing some very serious charges, and looking at the death penalty or life in prison if convicted. He could have easily stated something incorrectly and incriminated himself. He had been kept up to late hours in the morning, answering questions while his body was tired.

The detective asked my son if Mike Black had had any involvement with the shooting. My son told the detective that his cousin, Mike Black, had nothing to do with the shooting.

Then the detective said, "Was the shooting over a girl?"

My son answered, "I had no idea of what girl those dudes were talking about." He told the detective that if his girl, Tweetie, had cheated on him and he knew about it, they would no longer be together. Willie asked the detective if he would still be with his woman if she were cheating on him. Willie said that the detective stared at him with a peculiar look, as if he had been in a similar situation before that had involved a woman. Furthermore, there was an unconfirmed report of a jealous ex-girlfriend who had planted a seed of hate against Willie and wanted him killed! She was madly in love with Willie, and was upset that he showed no interest in her and had gotten a new girlfriend. Willie had quite a few ex-girlfriends who had never seemed to get over him. They always kept in touch with our family members, and wanted to know where he was and how he was doing.

PRISON

Later that night, the detective took my son to East Baton Rouge Parish Prison. Willie was facing capital murder charges: one count of first-degree murder and two counts of attempted first-degree murder. I thought that I would never see my son free again. They charged him with first-degree murder because there had been implications of premeditation. Several people at the party told the police that Willie and Mike Black had driven by and checked out the party in a white Jeep, playing very loud, booming music. The witnesses also stated that the cover to the Jeep had been on when they first drove by the party, but off when they returned. Furthermore, shortly after Willie and Mike Black returned to the party, the shooting occurred.

It was very depressing to hear Willie's name on television and to see it published in the local newspaper with murder charges. Every time they printed something in the paper about the incident, I would throw the newspaper into the trash. It seemed as though they would print every little thing incorrectly in the paper. The local newspaper even called my home and asked my son if he wanted to give his side of the story, but Willie declined. That year, murders in Baton Rouge were at an all-time high, and they even put Willie's name in the paper again to add to those statics. When my son was indicted, his name was yet again placed in the paper. By that time, I had had enough, and just stopped reading the newspaper for a while. I was just disgusted over the entire incident, and wished it had never happened. Willie told me that something really eerie happened while he was being processed at the prison, and receiving his prison clothing. A trustee, an older black man in his late sixties, was mopping the floor and kept staring at him.

He approached Willie and said, "I was around your age when I first came to prison, and you will never see the free world again for killing that boy."

My son said that it felt like a pile of bricks had landed on him. Then he began to wonder if he would become like the old man and never get out of prison. While in jail, he told me that while he slept there for the first few days, he could smell gunpowder in his dreams. The smell seemed so real that it would wake him in his sleep. I wrote him all the time when he was in jail, and told him how I thought I had failed as a mother. My son felt that I had done the best I could in raising him by myself. He said that the letters made him sad, and that he needed to stay strong while in prison. He wrote back saying not to write those kinds of letters, and that how I'd raised him had nothing to do with the shooting.

❖ ❖ ❖

My son told me about how some inmates managed to create crafty things in jail, and how some of them made coffee from cigarettes, pressed their clothes, and knitted skullcaps from silk underwear. They could make their clothes look like they had just come from the cleaners. Willie said that they would achieve this by placing their shirt and pants under a mattress that was set on a concrete slab, and sleep on their clothes for a couple of weeks or until they were satisfied with the creases. The skullcaps were made by stitching square shapes cut from silk underwear. They could get really creative with the colors and stitching. They even had their own jailhouse lingo: one very important term for snacks was "zoos." A saying that was universal in the jailhouse was, "Commissary is necessary." Zoos would be traded for cigarettes and skullcaps. However, Willie said that the prison food was very bland. Even the fried chicken did not have any seasoning on it. Willie was sick of eating the food after two weeks.

RELEASED FROM PRISON

Thirty days had passed, and my son could not believe that he was still in prison. So he called and asked me, "Ma, what is going on with the attorney?" The first lawyer we'd hired told my son that the best he could get him was a five-year sentence. Willie felt that he had done nothing wrong and did not want to spend another day in jail. We got another lawyer, and my son was released from prison. Thank God! He was cleared of all charges with the hard work of our attorney. The attorney did some amazing work to recover the gang members' gun. When police had questioned them, they had told the detectives that they did not have a gun. However, it was known on the streets that the gang members had thrown their gun away after they had left the scene of the shooting. I think my son would have been convicted if our attorney had not located their gun and linked the gang members to it.

Willie knew how difficult it had been to clear him of those charges and not get the death penalty or life in prison. He vowed to listen to me from then on! I told him that he needed to get out the game and join the Army.

I said, "All of your friends are dead, in jail, on drugs, or selling drugs."

He knew that I was telling him the truth. Mo' Money had gotten arrested a few times already; as I spoke, he was awaiting his sentencing from his last arrest and faced spending some serious time in prison. He had just bought himself a brand new drop-top Corvette and was sitting on top of the world. More so, Mike Black and Roe were heavily hooked on cocaine. Joining the Army was something my son did not want to do.

However, after spending a month out of jail, he told me, "Okay, Ma, I will join the Army."

I could not believe it, my son listened to me and enlisted in the service!

CHAPTER 13

MILITARY
FORT SILL

BASIC TRAINING

In 1990, my son kept his word and enlisted in the United States Army for four years. His first duty station was at Fort Sill, Oklahoma. He served his first two years in the military there. He almost participated in Desert Storm, but the war ended just as he was shipping out. One of the first things my son did when he joined the Army was sign up for the Montgomery G.I. Bill. The bill funded thirty-six months, or three years, of college tuition—whichever came first. My son attended night classes after his duties were done. A typical military day ran from 6:00 a.m. to 4:30 p.m., and included physical training. Willie decided not to use his G.I. Bill until his four-year military commitment was over. The Army also paid 75% of tuition for active-duty soldiers taking college classes. Even though Willie had left his homeboys and the environment he'd grown up in, some bad habits were hard to break. The drinking continued while he was in the military, and so did the fights. Willie explained to me that there were a lot of guys in the military from all sorts of backgrounds, cultures, and races, many of whom also came from bad environments with gangs, drug activity, and poor families. However, there were a few guys who grew up with silver spoons in their mouths, and joined the military to keep up a family tradition. Nonetheless, the fights constantly occurred, especially in basic training. There was probably a fight every weekend, and my son had his share of them, too.

MEED

During basic training, my son became friends with a guy named Meed from Florida. Willie identified with Meed because they both had a gold tooth and spoke with a southern slang. Meed was a short guy. He was about five foot seven, but was stocky and built like a tank. Meed was always ready to fight. My son told me of an incident that occurred during basic training: a group of white boys were gathered around talking in the barracks about their hometowns, and one guy said, "There are no niggers where I live."

Now, this guy was about six foot three, and muscularly built. He had been born and raised in the mountains of West Virginia. My son said that Meed stared at him with an, *it's about to go down* look, and they both walked over to the group of white boys.

Meed walked up to the guy from West Virginia and said, "Hey, man, what's up with you?"

The guy from West Virginia replied, "Hey, man, what's up with you, boy?"

Before the guy could finish pronouncing the word "boy," Meed punched him in the mouth, and they commenced fighting. While Meed was giving him a serious beat-down, my son said that he had Meed's back, just in case the other guys tried to jump in.

Then someone yelled, "The drill sergeant is coming," and everyone dispersed.

MEED'S PRANK

Meed and Willie always looked out for one another and constantly joked around. Once, Meed played a prank on Willie during the M-16 drills. Meed was in formation directly behind Willie, and kicked his M-16 out his hand. When the weapon hit the concrete floor, it made a very loud noise. What's more, a solider is never supposed to drop his weapon while in formation.

The drill sergeant heard the weapon hit the floor and yelled, "Scumbag, get down with your weapon and do pushups until I release the formation."

Meed had himself a good laugh that day, and my son promised Meed that he would pay him back. Meed continued doing things that soldiers in basic training were not allowed to do. He would find pay phones where he and Willie could call their girlfriends back home. They would sneak out of their barracks at night to a set of barracks where active-duty solders lived with pay phones. One of the drill sergeants began to pay close attention to Willie. His name was Drill Sergeant Kilpatrick. He pulled my son aside one day and told him that he thought Willie was a good person and a good soldier, but that he should choose his friends more wisely. Willie gave Drill Sergeant Kilpatrick's advice some serious thought.

KARMA

It was close to graduation, and the soldiers were getting their dress green military uniforms inspected by Drill Sergeant Kilpatrick and the commanding officer, himself. This was a serious inspection, and everything had to be perfect before the big graduation ceremony. While in the formation, Willie was positioned directly behind Meed. My son thought to himself, *Karma is real, and this is probably my last chance to get Meed back for kicking my weapon and embarrassing me during the M-16 drills.* Willie figured that if he did not do something then, there might not be another opportunity, because once they graduated from Basic Training, they'd be going their separate ways. My son told me that the kick had to be quick and precise, and he had only one chance to pull it off. He would have to do it once the drill sergeant and the commanding officer reached the last row, and their backs were turned to him. So when they made it to the last row and started inspecting the soldiers' uniforms, Willie eased up, kicked Meed's weapon out of his hand, and quickly moved back to his position in the formation.

The drill sergeant was outraged! He yelled out, "Drop with it and don't stop pushing until I get tired of hearing your freaking voice."

Willie said that he could hardly contain his laughter. Meed must have done a thousand pushups in his dress green uniform, and was put on extra duty in the mess hall. Meed had to spend the rest of his free time washing dishes until he graduated. But the soldier who had been standing in formation beside my son did not think that the prank was funny.

After the drill sergeant and the commanding officer walked away from the formation, he stepped to Willie and said, "This is the United States Army, and this inspection is a serious deal, and you do not need to be monkeying around during it."

My son said that he immediately punched him in the mouth, and they began to fight. Another soldier grabbed Willie around the neck from behind, and all of the other soldiers began to fight, also. The fighting continued until someone yelled that the drill sergeant was coming.

Later that day, Meed told my son, "Gat, you got me good."

GRIBB

My son met a very good friend named Gribb while stationed at Fort Sill. He and Gribb shared a room in the barracks during their first two years at Fort Sill. They even went on to be stationed at the same duty stations throughout their entire military careers. Gribb was the opposite of my son. Gribb was from a small town in Texas and was a few years younger than Willie. Gribb did not drink, smoke, or even curse, and was a very mild-mannered guy. My son told me that he and Gribb became really good friends, and Gribb invited him to his hometown to meet his family and friends.

However, one thing Gribb could not understand was why my son drank so much and was ready to fight all the time.

My son said that he would tell Gribb, "Cuz that's how I grew up, brah."

My son tried to get Gribb to have a beer with him, but Gribb would always say, "Man, go on with that bull corn, dog."

My son thought that that was so country and funny. He would tell Gribb to say "bullshit" instead of "bull corn," but Gribb never did.

Willie said that he started to see Gribb more as a little brother than a roommate. They did pretty much everything together while in the military. One particular thing Gribb would do that neither my son nor his friend paid much attention to.

Gribb would sometimes get headaches during the day. Sometimes, when Willie asked Gribb to shoot pool or play dominoes with him, Gribb said, "Not right now, dog, I got a bad headache."

My son thought nothing of it and figured that maybe Gribb was just tired after a long day of work. Besides, he usually took a nap during their lunch break. My son said he always teased Gribb when he took that nap by saying, "Yeah, dog, you got your girl pregnant back home; Lil' G is on the way, potna!"

Sadly, those headaches continued to plague Gribb throughout his life.

ADOPT A SOLDIER

An interesting incident occurred while Willie was in training at Fort Sill. It was Christmastime, and the Army had asked the soldiers to participate in "Adopt a Soldier for Christmas." The drill sergeants made it sound more fun than sitting alone in the barracks during Christmas, so Willie decided to try it out. Then the sergeant told him that he would be spending Christmas with a white family.

My son replied, "Come on, Drill Sergeant, give me a black family, man. I am gonna be bored out my mind there."

The sergeant replied, "Soldier, you do not get to choose the family."

The family that selected my son lived in Lawton, which was located right outside Fort Sill's gates. When Willie arrived at the family's house, he saw an older white couple, maybe in their late sixties, along with a younger couple that appeared to be in their late forties. My son told me that he said, "Hello," introduced himself, and stated the city and state where he lived. The older gentlemen introduced himself as Bill, and his wife, Sarah. Bill asked Willie what his job was in the military. My son told him about his job and the duties that he performed.

Bill told Willie that he was a retired military veteran, and that his wife was a retired school teacher. Bill mentioned some of the things he had done in the military, and the places he had been stationed, and then introduced his son, Jeff, and Jeff's wife, Julie.

Jeff and Julie owned a restaurant. Willie thought that that was really cool because he hoped to own a business himself one day. He wanted to ask the couple a thousand questions about starting and maintaining their business. I guess you could say that the cat got his tongue, because he could not bring himself to ask them any questions. Willie told everyone that it was nice to meet them, and asked if he could watch television. The men replied, "Sure," and also that they thought some games were about to begin. My son sat down in the living room to watch television, and everyone in the house was very quiet. Then Bill told my son that some of his grandchildren were on their way over to his house, and that they were around his age. Willie thought to himself, *Great, some heavy metal punk rockers or county hillbillies are on the way to ruin my football games.*

However, when the grandchildren—three girls and one boy—arrived, they did not appear to be heavy metal fans or hillbillies. They called Willie to the back room where they were listening to rap music, dancing, drinking alcohol, and having a blast. Willie went to the back room and had a great time. More so, my son was glad that he went, after all.

MALCOLM X

While he was in the military, Willie had a lot of free time and began to read books. One book that had a positive impact on his life was *The Autobiography of Malcolm X: As Told to Alex Haley*. It was surprising how my son became interested in learning about Malcolm X. The movie, *Malcolm X,* by Spike Lee was about to come out in theaters. Plenty of shirts and caps were being sold to promote the movie. My son was home visiting on military leave one winter when he told me that he had walked into a convenience store wearing a Malcolm X beanie.

An older black lady walked up to him as he was purchasing some beer, stared him in the eye, and said, "I see you are wearing the X cap. Do you know anything about Malcolm X?"

Before my son could respond, the lady turned around and walked out of the store. Willie said that he would not have had much to say in response, and he felt really bad and hungry to know about Malcolm X. When my son returned to the military base, he purchased Malcolm X's autobiography. Willie was inspired so much by the book that he stopped drinking alcohol and began to eat healthier. He became a more positive and ambitious person. It helped him obtain knowledge, wisdom, and understanding. He saw a lot of Malcolm's troubled background as being similar to his own. My son felt that he could do anything that he challenged himself to do, and obtain whatever he wanted in life if he put his mind to it.

CHAPTER 14

MILITARY
KOREA

SHAREIFF

In September of 1992, Willie and Tweetie were still dating. He had just received orders to deploy to Korea for one year. He and Tweetie had been together since high school, and had their first child. It was a boy! My son was so happy that the baby was a boy; he even thought Tweetie was pulling his leg about it being a boy. Willie had hoped that Tweetie would have a boy; he had major plans for his son. They named him Sharieff. Willie had a difficult time deciding on a name for his son. It was his first child, and he wanted his name to really be special. He bought all kinds of books to help him choose a name. However, every name he came up with, Tweetie did not like.

Finally, he asked her, "What do you think about Sharieff Kalieff?"

She said, "Okay, but drop Kalieff and add Marcel."

My son did not like the middle name that Tweetie wanted to use, but since she had accepted the first name, he left well enough alone.

Willie and Tweetie's relationship was off and on after he joined the military. The phone calls and letters that came once a week were not enough to fill the voids of each other's absence. The long distance thing was just not working out. My son saw Tweetie whenever he came home on military leave, and Tweetie visited Willie when he arrived at his first duty station. He hid Tweetie in his room at the barracks, and his roommate stayed in another soldier's room while Tweetie was there. The other soldiers also looked out for them, because no girls were allowed to stay in a male soldier's room. They spent a weekend together, going to the movies and touring the base. She enjoyed the military environment and culture, as well as the surrounding area.

CAR JACKING

Willie was away in the military when Sharieff was born, and had just received orders to deploy to Korea for a one-year tour shortly after his son's birth. My son took leave from the military to come home and see his son and family before he went overseas.

Unfortunately, Tweetie lived in the same neighborhood as the gang member my son had shot and killed. However, Willie was determined to see his son before he left for Korea. Willie asked his cousin, Squirk, if he could use his car to go and see his son. My son always said that Squirk had missed his calling and should have gone into boxing: he was known on the streets as "One Hitta Quitta." He was not a very big guy, and stood about five feet, nine inches tall, and weighed a solid two hundred pounds. However, he could knock out guys much bigger than him with one punch.

Squirk's car was probably not a good choice because it really stood out. It was a 1976 cream-colored Oldsmobile with gold Truespoke rims, Vogue tires, and ragtop cover. It also had a booming sound system in it. Willie felt a little uneasy about the trip, so he took his 9mm pistol and an extra clip with him. It was about 8:00 p.m. when Willie arrived at Tweetie's mother's house. He put the gun in his waistband at the small of his back and the extra clip into his pocket. Tweetie and her mother were at the house along with Willie and Tweetie's newborn son. Tweetie told Willie that their son was asleep in the back bedroom, and that she would go and get him. She returned with Sharieff and handed him to Willie. Willie saw and held his son for the first time and was overjoyed!

My son had been there for about thirty minutes when he heard loud music coming from vehicles outside. Tweetie peeked out the front window and said that some gang members were out there. Willie thought to himself, *Damn, here we go again!*

Tweetie yelled out, "They are stealing the car!"

Willie jumped up and pulled the gun from his waistband. He ejected a bullet into the chamber and headed for the door.

Tweetie dashed over, screaming frantically, "No, no, don't go out there," then dove to the floor and clutched my son's leg so he could not get out the door. It was like she was a professional football player and was going to prevent Willie from gaining another yard. However, my son was near a window and could see the carjacker inside the vehicle. Willie had a clear view of him, and raised the window to shoot the carjacker as he tried to hotwire the car. My son said that he had him right in his pistol's sight!

However, before he could squeeze off some rounds, Tweetie's mom came over and grabbed the gun. She wrestled with Willie, clutching the gun with all her might, screaming for my son to not shoot, and pleading for Willie to give her the gun! She and my son tussled for the gun for a few minutes, and then she said, "Willie Gat, no one is out there. They have already stolen the car and left."

My son said that he released the gun to her and sat down on the couch with his head in his hands, in utter disbelief. Not only was the car stolen, but Willie's jacket and wallet, too. That incident really put him in a bind.

Willie had just bought a brand-new New Orleans Saints Starter jacket, and he was pissed. My son had to get his driver's license and other military things taken care of before he flew overseas. The following day, the neighbors informed Tweetie and her mom that the gang members had had their house surrounded with the intent of shooting the driver of the vehicle if he had come outside.

When Willie told Squirk about the incident, his cousin said, "Don't worry brah, them fools gon' get they issue!"

THE FLIGHT

Willie hated to leave his newborn son and head off to Korea for a year. He wanted to be there to hear his son utter the word "dada," and to see him crawl around on the floor. He wanted to see him waddle around the floor in his walker, and bang on his toys. He was also still mad about the carjacking and could not get the incident out his head. Things could have turned out really badly that night; someone could have been killed or seriously injured, and to top it all off, his newborn son had been put in harm's way! My son had serious payback on his mind. Willie told me that the flight to Korea was so long that it gave him too much time to think and play back the incident in his head. Nonetheless, the flight over there was a once-in-a-lifetime experience for him, and he was looking forward to seeing another part of the world. He had never dreamed of flying that far in his life. I told him to call me and let me know how the flight had gone as soon as he landed in Korea. When I spoke to my son, he told me that the flight had not bothered him, though he was not looking forward to living in Korea for a year. He had flown on the military's big jumbo jet, the C-130. He told me that he had fallen asleep during the flight over there, and when he woke, he had still been flying. Willie said that the entire flight had been fifteen hours long, and something really breathtaking had occurred on the flight. My son told me that the captain came on the intercom and told everyone to look out their windows. Willie was fortunate enough to have a window seat, and was amazed to see these humongous mountains covered with snow. My son said that his mouth flew open and his eyes almost popped out of his head! Willie looked at the mountains from top to bottom and admired the earth's beauty. He said that they were so tall that they were literally in the clouds!

The captain told everyone on the plane, "Ladies and gentleman, we are now flying over the Alps Mountains!"

My son told me that it was an incredible feeling.

CAMP CASEY

When my son received orders to report to Korea, so did his old barracks buddy, Gribb. Willie told me about the time when he and Gribb were waiting in formation to hear the sergeant call their names and let them know where in Korea they would be spending the next year. All of the soldiers had joked about not wanting to be sent up north near the demilitarized zone, or DMZ. Soldiers hated to be sent to the DMZ, which lay between North Korea and South Korea, because there was not much shopping, clubbing, or much else to do there. The soldiers stationed there were usually pissed off all the time, and tension was very high. The soldiers there usually spent most of their time drinking and getting into fights. However, being sent farther south was no paradise, either. The ratio of men to women was one hundred men to every one woman. My son said that the soldiers acted a fool at the clubs over women. He also said that women loved being stationed there: they got to be queens for a year while in Korea. Willie said that when the sergeant called for him to report to Camp

Casey, he was relieved. Camp Casey was not in the southern part of Korea, but it was a whole lot better than living near the DMZ. There were plenty of clubs, shops, and people at its location. However, his friend, Gribb, was sent farther north, near the DMZ. That was the first time they had ever been separated during their military career.

My son told me that Gribb just put his head down and said, "Aw, man, dog, that's bull corn!"

That was the first time that Gribb said "bull corn" that Willie did not find funny.

My son told his friend, "Don't worry about it, dog. The year would be over before you know it, G. And we will be back in the States."

When Willie made it to his barracks, he noticed that all of the soldiers had a calendar of Korea on their walls. The country was numbered with 365 blocks, each representing one day of the year. The very last block led to a plane waiting to fly the soldier back to the United States. Each soldier colored in the blocks as the days went by. Willie said that it was very depressing to see your calendar in the beginning, but a joy at the end.

My son enjoyed learning about Korean culture, as well as doing some shopping over there. He also said that the Koreans had all the latest trends in their shops; they even knew and had all the latest rap music. Willie said that those tapes really came in handy: listening to current music from back home really made you feel good. My son said that while they mostly played dominos to pass the time, the best thing that he and some fellow soldiers did on the weekends was watch recordings of the *Martin Lawrence* television show. One soldier's wife recorded about a month's worth of *Martin Lawrence* episodes on a tape to mail to her husband. Willie said that they all waited for that package to arrive.

My son said that when the soldier named Wilcox announced, "Get the popcorn ready, the package has arrived," everyone got excited and prepared to watch Martin that night. Martin's show was already a hilarious comedy, but when you are overseas and not privileged to watching it all the time, it becomes ten times as funny when you do.

Willie was also shocked to see how much Koreans knew about American culture and our country. My son said that whenever they were in Seoul, they used cabs to get around the city. He told me about this one taxi cab driver who was very knowledgeable about the United States: he said that if my son and another soldier called out any state in America, he could name where it was located and give the name of its capital city. It was really amazing how fast he could do it, and how much he knew about America.

On one of his trips to Seoul, Willie watched a live dancing show and visited some historical sites. He took lots of pictures and videotaped the entire event. However, my son said that being stationed in Korea was a little bit nerve-racking because though you constantly heard that North Korea was going to invade South Korea, but no one knew when, so everyone had to be ready at all times. Whenever my son went to sleep at night, that thought was in the back of his mind: *Is tonight going to be the night it goes down, when the North invades the South?*

A few months after my son arrived in Korea, he received a letter along with pictures of his baby boy from Tweetie. She wrote that someone had shot the gang members who had stolen Squirk's car. Willie had a feeling that those fools would get their issue. He was also excited to get those pictures of his son from Tweetie. She would send some just about every month so Willie could see his son crawling around on the floor and trying to take his very first steps.

COLLEGE COURSES

After duty hours, my son was able to take a few classes and obtain college credits while in Korea. Willie told me that there were a few schools from the United States located on-post for the soldiers. My son was able to take classes from Central Texas College and University of Maryland at College Park. He did not even need to use his G.I. Bill. The Army paid 75% of the tuition for active-duty soldiers who were taking classes. My son said that his unit worked with him and other soldiers, and allowed transportation from the field so they could make it to their classes at night. Even though this great opportunity was available, not many soldiers took advantage of it. My son said that taking classes was one of the best things he could have done while stationed in Korea. He was not postponing his degree, it kept him busy, and the time went by faster. Willie said that another big thing he was able to accomplish while in Korea was saving money. He was no longer drinking at the time, and did not need much money in Korea. His military checks were just being deposited into the bank and never being touched for one whole year, except to provide baby things for his newborn son back home.

SKINHEAD

My son said that he literally came face-to-face with racial hatred while in the Army. He had already spent two years in the military, and had never encountered anything like this before in his life. Willie was living with his unit in the barracks. It was a close-knit environment. One morning, after physical training, he went to take a shower. My son said that he was exhausted and felt like he had run ten miles that morning. As he approached the shower, a white soldier named Alden was leaving it. There were also several other soldiers brushing their teeth, showering, and taking care of personal hygiene. Willie said that as he lifted his head, he saw something that made his blood boil!

Alden had an enormous black tattoo on his chest of a massive oak tree with people hanging from it!

The tree resembled the large ones you saw on slave plantations. My son said that the anger immediately set in all over his face as he and Alden walked toward one another.

My son asked the soldier, "Who are those people hanging from that muthafuckin' tree?"

Alden paused for several minutes and replied, "They are criminals."

My son said that he had hoped that Alden would say the people were "niggers" or "black people" so he could have beaten his brains out!

Willie had just barely gotten out of serious trouble back home, and knew that if he physically harmed that soldier, he would most likely be dishonorably discharged from the Army, and his career would pretty much be over. However, Alden did not say or do anything to provoke a fight. My son said that he later heard from other soldiers that they thought Alden was a skinhead because he and other white soldiers with shaved heads would often have private meetings. They often wore black boots with white or red shoelaces, and suspenders. My son often struck up conversations with Alden to see if he would respond with racist comments, but he never did. Alden enjoyed discussing his ancestry and the Pilgrims who had landed in the New England region where he lived. Alden told Willie that he loved to listen to "Gangster Rap," and that NWA (Niggaz With Attitude) was his favorite group.

My son asked him, "Why do you love that type of music so much?" but before he could answer, Willie told him, "I know why you love it—you love it because they rap about blacks killing blacks. That shit is music to your ears, huh?"

Alden remained silent and did not comment.

My son said that his suspicions were proven correct during formation one day. It was Friday, and sometimes the sergeant in charge of the platoon would give the soldier with the best uniform the rest of the day off. That morning, after Sergeant Schmidt walked through the formation and inspected everyone's uniforms, he told Alden to step out of the formation and take the rest of the day off. The facial expressions of the other soldiers' were priceless. They looked as though someone had splashed cold water on their faces. Alden's uniform was wrinkled and shabby from top to bottom; it looked like he had just grabbed his uniform from the laundry basket and put it on. His boots were adequate, but not shiny. There were plenty of soldiers with spit-shined boots and freshly pressed uniforms standing in formation.

Willie could not believe what he had just witnessed, and could not keep his mouth shut. My son yelled out, "That's messed up, Sarge, his uniform looks like shit!"

However, the sergeant ignored Willie and walked away from the formation. My son said that Sergeant Schmidt sent a message to everyone in the formation that day, and that message was, "I got Alden's back!"

CHAPTER 15

MILITARY
FORT HOOD

MARRIAGE

My son and Gribb received orders to report to Fort
Hood, Texas, on October 1, 1993. Willie and Gribb both
married their girlfriends from back home after returning
from Korea. They were so glad to be back in the United
States. My son said that spending a year in Korea had
helped convince him to propose to Tweetie. He and
Tweetie got their first apartment in Copperas Cove,
Texas, a few miles outside Fort Hood's military base.

Gribb and his wife, Lena, got an apartment in Killeen, Texas, which was also right outside the military base. The two brides even became friends and got to know one another very well.

VIDOR, TX.

My son remembered a bad experience he and Tweetie had in Vidor, Texas, where her car broke down. Willie and Tweetie had just gotten married, and they were driving to Fort Hood, where Willie was stationed. Tweetie was trailing my son's vehicle, and all of a sudden, her car stalled and died on I-10 West. Conveniently, there was a repair shop a few hundred feet away, so they were able to push her car to the shop with the help of a gentleman. My son told me that the mechanic at the shop gave him bad vibes from the start: the mechanic immediately started talking big money even though he hadn't even looked under the hood yet. After the mechanic finally took a look under the hood, he began to speculate what the problem might be, and suggested that the repair work could cost thousands of dollars. Now, Tweetie's vehicle was an older model Toyota Celica, and was probably worth five hundred dollars.

My son said that by this time, his blood was starting to boil! So he told the mechanic to tell him the problem and the exact cost to fix it. The mechanic said that he really did not know yet, and that he needed to check out a few more things, first. Tweetie began to see the frustration and anger on Willie's face, and noticed that he was very irritated with the mechanic. Tweetie was also nervous because she knew that Willie had a loaded 9mm in his vehicle, so she tried to calm her husband down and told him that they should just go somewhere else. The mechanic adjusted a few things, and the car started for a few seconds, but began to knock and shake until it died again. The mechanic then claimed to know what the problem was, and gave Willie an estimate of twenty-five hundred dollars to fix it!

My son asked the man, "Are you crazy? Where is the nearest truck rental company in town?"

My son rented a bobtail truck and hauled Tweetie's car out of that mechanic's garage to Fort Hood. He took Tweetie's car to a vehicle repair shop near the military base and explained to the mechanic there what had happened in Vidor. He popped the hood, and about thirty seconds later, Tweetie's car was humming like a bird.

Willie asked him, "What was the problem?"

The mechanic there told my son that he did not know what the mechanic in Vidor initially did to fix the problem, but the only thing left to do was correctly connect the spark plug wires. The mechanic told Willie that the spark plug wires had been installed wrong; they were connected to the wrong spark plugs, so the car was misfiring!

My son was elated and knew that he had been right about that mechanic in Vidor being shady. He asked the mechanic how much they owed him.

The mechanic said, "Nothing. You had a rough time getting here, and I only switched the spark plug wires."

My son thanked the man and told him that he wished that there were more mechanics like him.

My son and his new bride were not at Fort Hood for very long before they got into a fight. They had just arrived on the base, and checked into a suite for the day. Willie said that the two of them were yelling up a storm, and the baby was crying because of the commotion. Then there was a knock on the door. My son went over to look out the window and saw military police everywhere. They were behind cars with their guns drawn and posted around the door. My son opened the door, and the MP told him that someone had reported a disturbance at this location.

My son told the MP, "No, sir, not here."

The MP said, "Sir, I need you to step outside and move away from the door."

My son said, "Hey, man, what the hell is going on?"

The MP said, "Sir, step outside and put your hands behind your head!"

My son said, "Man, for what? I haven't done shit!"

The MP grabbed Willie, handcuffed him, and hauled him to the other side of the building while demanding, "Where is the weapon? Where is the weapon?"

For some crazy reason, my son was still packing pistols and had taken a gun into the suite. Someone must have seen him with it, heard him and Tweetie arguing, and called the Military Police.

The police got Tweetie and their son out the room and confiscated Willie's gun. Then they arrested my son and took him to jail. He was released after everything was revealed to be a misunderstanding.

However, he and Tweetie separated after that incident, and she caught the next flight home to Baton Rouge.

The breakup did not last long; Tweetie came back within a month.

Shortly after they got settled at Fort Hood, my son had to spend a month in California for desert training. He was not excited about that assignment at all. He had just spent a year in Korea away from his family, and now he had to turn right back around and leave again. My son said that he remembered that Tweetie was having a tough time handling everything alone with the baby.

My son said that he was faced with a big decision during his last year in the Army. He was contemplating whether he should leave the military or reenlist. Everyone he worked with in the Army was telling him to reenlist. They told him that he would have a hard time finding a job in the civilian world because no one hired a veteran unless he had worked in the medical field or had been a high-ranking officer in the service. Tweetie also wanted him to reenlist in the Army. But he now had a family to support and did not want to make the wrong choice. My son said that he had spoken with a few veterans who lived in the area, all of whom had recently decided to get out of the military. They all were struggling, and told Willie that they wished they had stayed in the service. However, the low pay, slow promotions, and the possibility of being gone for training or deployment weighed heavily on his decision.

My son came up with a plan: he decided to obtain a commercial driving license and drive trucks after discharging from the Army. He figured that driving trucks would be a safe route to pursue, and getting hired as a veteran would not be a problem in the trucking industry. He studied very hard, and passed the test and obtained the CDL license. He also made sure that he had a truck-driving job lined up before he got out of the Army. Willie and Tweetie had their eye on moving to either Atlanta, Georgia, or Houston, Texas. They decided that wherever my son landed a job was where they would move. He search diligently for a job, and was hired by a food supply company in Houston.

On October 1, 1994, Willie discharged from the Army and moved with his family to Houston.

CHAPTER 16

LOSSES
GLOOM

TRUCK DRIVER

Willie, Tweetie, and their son got an apartment in Southwest Houston. Willie loved Houston. He enjoyed seeing the tall, beautiful buildings and the highway infrastructure. He liked the local sports franchises. The Houston Rockets and the Houston Oilers were in town when my son moved there. However, he and Tweetie did not like where some of the schools were located. A lot of the schools in Houston were located right off busy streets. Willie and Tweetie were accustomed to the schools back home in Louisiana, which were located in neighborhoods. Tweetie did not like Houston, and wanted to live back home in Baton Rouge.

A Greek family owned the food company for which my son worked. The husband, wife, son, daughters, and sons-in-law all worked for the company. They had eighteen-wheelers and bobtail trucks, and they delivered food supplies all over the United States. They sold a variety of frozen and canned foods, and specialized in cheeses, tomato sauces, olives, meats, and seasonings. My son agreed to drive bobtail trucks locally for the company, and was expected to drive out of town one day out the week. The old man ran the company with a tight fist. He was also a military veteran and was excited to see Willie working for his company. My son said that he thought the old man knew that he had no experience driving bobtail trucks, but let him deliver their products anyway. They knew that my son was originally from Louisiana, and was fresh out the military, so he did not know his way around the city. Houston is a very large city, and my son had to learn how to drive that truck and navigate the city very fast. Willie said that they gave him a key map and told him to just call the office if he had any problems. My son said that there were plenty of nights when he returned to the yard to find everyone gone. He had gotten lost a few times, but made all of his deliveries within a reasonable time. Luckily, my son is a quick learner, and within a month he was driving around the city and surrounding areas without the key map. The old man did not care how long Willie stayed out delivering the products, just as long as all the items got delivered. Later, Willie soon found out why the old man was happy to have a young guy working for his company: the company had a terrible time keeping drivers because it expected them to deliver and stock the products at a low wage. My son said that he constantly lobbied for an increase in pay. However, the company would not give the truck drivers an extra dime. They gave their drivers a yearly raise that did not amount to much, and the loads and the routes just got bigger and longer.

Willie was excited about raising his son. He knew how important a father figure was to a boy. My son wanted to give his boy the father that Willie had never had. He was on the road a lot, working very hard to support his family, and was not able to attend college. Willie wanted to be the best father that he could, and devoted himself 100% to his family. However, his marriage was shaky from the start, with separations occurring at least three times during their short, year-and-a-half-old marriage. The last time they separated, Willie had just returned from delivering products to Austin. He was very tired that day from having worked for twelve hours. When he returned home from Austin that evening, Tweetie and his son were gone. She had packed all of her and their son's things, and had driven back to Baton Rouge in the new 1994 Jeep they had just purchased. After my son walked through the apartment and noticed that Tweetie had packed up and left, he was furious! He immediately grabbed the keys to her car and drove to Louisiana. My son said that he drove straight to Tweetie's mother's apartment. He figured that it would be the first place that she would go. Once he made it there, he saw their Jeep and parked beside it. My son walked around the vehicle and paced back and forth in the parking lot, hoping that Tweetie would come outside, because he knew that she was near a window, watching him.

Nevertheless, Tweetie did not come outside, and made no attempt to contact Willie. My son kept the spare set of keys to the new vehicle with him; after he realized that Tweetie was not coming out to talk to him, he left the keys to her car under the floor mat on the driver's side and drove away in their new Jeep. My son drove to my house and explained to me what had happened. I told him to stay the night and get some rest, because he was too tired to turn right back around and drive to Houston. My son told me that he would drink a cup of coffee and head back to Houston, because he had to be at work early the next day.

ORANGE, TX.

My son was just about to enter Orange, Texas, on I-10 heading west, when he noticed that a police car with two officers inside was trailing him, so he signaled to move over into the far right lane. After my son moved into the lane, the police car pulled behind him and put its flashers and siren on. My son told me that he then pulled over onto the shoulder, wondering why the police had stopped him. He had not been speeding, nor had he done anything illegal.

Willie said that he was approached by a police officer with a flashlight, and was asked to step out of his vehicle.

My son recalled that that section of roadway was not well illuminated, and was undeveloped with many trees on both sides. After my son stepped out his vehicle, the other officer got out of the police car and approached him. The officer asked my son for his license and insurance. They both told my son that he had a very nice Jeep. While one of the officers ran Willie's license, the other one continued to chat with my son.

He asked Willie, "So, where are you coming from at 1:00 in the morning on a Tuesday night?"

My son told the officer, "I had to visit my relatives in Baton Rouge."

The officer said, "Well, buddy you would be surprised at how many people we pull over for smuggling drugs from Louisiana to Houston."

My son asked the officer, "Why did you all pull me over?"

The officer replied, "Well, we pulled you over because you made a suspicious lane change."

When the other officer came back, he shouted, "Hey, man, what the heck happened in Louisiana? You have some serious charges here, buddy!"

My son responded, "Man, those charges are in the past, and I'm done with that."

The officer said, "Okay, but we have a proposition for you. We have a K-9 in our squad car, and we are gonna give you two options: option one would be for my partner and I to search your vehicle; option two would be for us to get out the K-9 and let him sniff your vehicle."

My son said that he chose option one. He did not want that dog out, and told the officers to go ahead and check his vehicle.

The officer replied, "I figured you would choose that one."

My son said that they brought out their tools and thoroughly checked his vehicle. They unscrewed anything that could be unscrewed and found nothing. My son said that by the time he made it home that night, he was exhausted and thought that his rights had been violated! He also later discovered that some of the things that the officers had unscrewed in his trunk never bolted down securely again. No matter how hard he tried to fix it, it was never the same!

DIVORCE

Unfortunately, in 1995, Willie filed for a divorce. He and Tweetie did not work things out this time like they had done in the past. The divorce was a difficult experience, but it gave my son relief and allowed him to move on with his life. Thankfully, it was not an ugly divorce, and Tweetie did not contest it.

Ironically, they had dated for longer than they stayed married. They had been together during and after high school for approximately five years. Tweetie moved back home to Baton Rouge, and Willie had to watch his son grow up without a male figure in the home. This was the hardest thing for him to deal with from the divorce. Willie tried as much as possible to stay in his son's life. He knew how important that was to a young man, especially a black male: the odds are already against him, and no additional obstacles need to be added to his life. This was one concept that my son said that Tweetie did not understand.

Willie always told Tweetie, "If you leave and try to raise our son by yourself, you will mess him up, because it takes a man to raise a man."

DADDY PAST

My son's divorce really happened at a bad time. Daddy was in the hospital and was not doing well.

Unfortunately, Daddy died at the age of seventy-two from a stroke. My son was dealing with the loss of my father at the time of his divorce. The divorce really left a bitter taste in his mouth after he had tried so hard to make the marriage work. Willie was real close to my Daddy, and saw him as his own father figure.

Willie never remarried after his divorce. My son dated plenty of good women, but he would always find a reason why he thought a marriage with one of them would end in divorce. For example, if the woman had children, Willie disagreed with the way she raised her kids. Most of the women tended to let their kids do whatever they wanted, and not discipline them at all. Other things that bothered him were women who were too bossy or who fussed too much, let their families run their lives, or were not ambitious enough. The one thing Willie said all the time was, "They do not know when to shut up and be quiet."

I had hoped that my son would marry a girl he had met and dated in Houston. He brought her home for the family to meet, and everyone really liked her. I thought that she would have been good for him; I could see how much she loved and cared for my son. Willie could do nothing wrong in her eyes. He did ask me for my opinion on marrying her, but I decided not to tell him if he should or should not. I had learned my lesson from his first marriage, because I had told him to marry Tweetie since she was the mother of his child. Sadly, their marriage had been a total disaster from the start. Their marriage probably would have made it if their families had not intervened. Willie had grown up fast and had had big responsibilities from an early age. He had been forced to grow up that way. I do not recall Tweetie growing up as fast as my son had. He was twenty-two years old and she was only nineteen years of age when they got married. Maybe they were just too young. That probably was the main factor in their marriage not working out. My son did say one very important lesson he learned about getting married was that, "You are not only getting a new wife, but a new family, too!"

CHAPTER 17

BACHELOR
PARTY TIME

CLUBBING

After the divorce, Willie went back to college, but started drinking again and going out to the clubs. My youngest son, Gerrod, was starting to get into trouble at home, so Willie decided to let his younger brother move in with him, thinking that a change of environment would be good for him, and that with any luck, he could get his rap career going in Houston. Gerrod looked up to his older brother and pretty much listened to him about most things. So Gerrod, who no longer wanted to be called by his real name and went instead by O.G. Red, moved in with Willie in Southwest Houston.

My two sons clubbed from Monday to Sunday. They partied hard on the weekends, barbecuing, drinking, clubbing, and meeting girls.

Willie's neighbor said, "Hey man, what do you put in your food to get all those pretty women over there?"

My son laughed and replied, "It's got Louisiana flava in it, brah."

My son said that the clubs in Houston were jam-packed every night of the week. Each club had a certain night that people attended. Willie and Gerrod had a great time together, and they both loved to make one another laugh about things that had happened throughout the day. It was almost like two comedians living together, having a blast. I would get so nervous when my sons came home to visit. They would go straight to the old neighborhood, Rockwood, to hang out and hook up with their cousins and homeboys. The neighborhood changed so much over the years. There is probably a crack house on every street, now. My sons would be out in the streets all night, and would not make it to my house until the wee hours of the morning.

Later, when they woke up to eat breakfast, I would say to them, "Y'all should be ashamed of yourselves for not coming to see me before hanging out in those streets all night. Besides, ain't nothing but trouble in those streets at that time of morning, and I know you all were not drinking on that road, driving from Houston!"

They would both just look at one another and start laughing, then say, "Man, Mama know she need to stop trippin'."

Back in Houston, Gerrod, using his street name O.G. Red, entered different rap contests at clubs and rocked the audience. He had also gotten a job at a local nursery and was doing quite well. However, Gerrod loved to smoke marijuana and began to hang out with gangsters from the Southwest. Willie said that Gerrod had started posting up on corners in Houston and was running the streets, hard.

Willie told his brother, "Man, I did not bring you out here to get in the game! I got out the game and do not want it around me, or for you to get in it!"

However, Gerrod did not listen to his brother and got deeper into the game. He was arrested so often that Willie got tired of picking him up from Harris County Jail. So Willie sent Gerrod back to Baton Rouge after the last time he was arrested.

COLLEGE PARTY

My son told me one night that he decided to go to a local sports bar and hang out for a little while. On the way, he noticed a lot of nice-looking young ladies going into a building, so he stopped to check it out. The doorman told him that there was a college party going on inside, and that anyone could go in. My son paid the cover and went inside. Willie said that the place was jam-packed, and everyone was having a great time drinking, dancing, and socializing. My son told me that he had a few beers and started mingling with the young ladies there, and danced to a few songs. Maybe an hour or two had passed, and my son said that he noticed that the crowd was starting to look more thuggish as the night went on. So he began to pay more attention to his surroundings and the vibe of the crowd.

My son said that before you knew it, them "fools" started throwing up gang signs and waving their guns in the air, gunshots rang out in the parking lot. Everyone inside the club began to head towards the front door.

Then someone yelled, "He is about to shoot into the club!"

Everyone inside the club got on the floor, and my son got down on one knee. The crowd at the front door started running back into the club and created a stampede. The women were hollering, screaming, and falling all over one another. My son said that one really big, fat girl fell on top of him. She slammed right on his shoulder and dislocated it! My son said it felt as though she had jumped from the top rope of a wrestling ring; the force of her impact was tremendous!

Willie said that he had never felt pain like that before in his entire life! He rolled the big girl off of himself, stood up, and walked to the back of the club.

My son said that he was in so much pain that his ears were ringing. He looked over at his shoulder and it was literally almost next to his jaw.

Willie said that people were looking at his shoulder with their mouths open in disbelief, but no one stopped to help him because they were running away from the gunfire.

My son managed to walk to a corner away from the chaos. As he walked, he gently tried to move his shoulder, but it did not budge. Willie said that all he could think was, *I have to push it back in place to stop the pain.*

So he pushed a little harder, then a little harder, but it did not move!

Then he got angry and pushed with all his might, and his shoulder snapped back into place!

He said that the pain went away immediately, and he was so relieved.

My son said that he still could not believe that he had been able to put his shoulder back in place himself. Finally, the police arrived and restored order.

Willie went to the doctor to make sure that his shoulder was okay. The doctor told him that he must have pushed it back in place, and that everything was all right. The doctor also took x-rays, and they were good.

GEE GEE

Willie became friends with an ex-stripper named Gee Gee from California, and who lived in his apartment complex. He told me she was about twenty-one years old, tall, slender, and gorgeous. They would have drinks, listen to music, and party together at his apartment. However, she constantly wanted Willie to take her out to the club for drinks and to shoot pool. My son said that for some reason, he just did not feel comfortable about taking her to the club with him.

One Sunday night, when they were hanging out and drinking in his apartment, Gee Gee started up again about Willie taking her out to the club. Willie said, "Okay, let's go to the club nearby and shoot some pool."

My son figured that since it was Sunday, it would probably be a slow night at this particular club. They arrived at the club, bought some drinks, and got a table to shoot pool. They were having a good time; Gee Gee would dance to the music between her pool shots. Three guys began shooting pool at the table next to theirs. Willie figured from the way they were dressed that they were probably drug dealers from out of town. They were wearing what appeared to be Versace shirts, lots of jewelry, gator shoes, and Dobbs hats. They did not like that Willie was taking the pool rack from their table when it came time for him to rack his pool balls. The club manager noticed this and came over to place another pool rack on Willie and Gee Gee's table.

The club closed early on Sunday nights, and as Willie and Gee Gee were leaving, they heard a commotion at the front door. The bouncers were engaged in a fight with the three guys who had shot pool next to them. The bouncers beat them badly, and pulled their shirts over their heads while punching and kicking them. The guys stood up from the floor, pulled their shirts from over their heads, and saw Willie standing there as they wobbled out the club. As my son and Gee Gee approached Willie's vehicle, they heard a car speeding their way—then gunshots rang out!

Willie yelled at Gee Gee, "Get down!"

Gee Gee was so scared that she crawled under Willie's vehicle. My son opened his car door and dove onto the floor.

That night, Willie did not have a pistol with him and was trapped!

Glass shattered everywhere in his vehicle, and my son thought that tonight would be the night that he died!

All of a sudden, my son heard police sirens, but bullets were still hitting his vehicle. Once the sound of gunfire subsided, he got out to see if anyone had been hit.

Gee Gee crawled out from beneath Willie's vehicle, crying, screaming, and shaking. The police were in hot pursuit of the gunmen, who shot at them as they sped out the club's parking lot. The police eventually caught the guys and arrested them that night.

Later, Willie spoke with the club manager about the incident. The manager explained that everything had been recorded on video, but that he could not show Willie the tape. The manager also asked if Willie recalled that he had brought the extra pool rack to his table.

My son told the manager, "Yeah, I do remember you placing a pool rack at my table."

The manager said, "I did that because those guys looked at you really crazy when you took the pool rack from their table without asking them to borrow it."

My son said, "Yeah, but I don't think the guys were shooting at me over the pool rack."

Willie told the manager that the guys had seen him standing there and must have thought that he had been one of the guys who beat them when their shirts had been pulled over their heads.

The manager said, "The commotion at the front door was over the guys wanting to reenter the club after we told them the club was closed. They wanted to come back into the club for the girl that was with you."

The manager also told Willie that he had video of her allegedly performing sexual acts with one of those guys in the restroom. It was later confirmed that the guys were from out of town somewhere near Dallas, Texas. The guys would later stand trial and be sentenced to prison for the shooting.

CHAPTER 18

GRADUATION
SUCCEEDED

CIVIL ENGINEERING DEGREE

After Willie divorced Tweetie, he changed his major from criminal justice to civil engineering. He wanted to design roads and bridges. He was really focused and wanted to take on something challenging. He visited different colleges to get information on their engineering programs, but the counselors told him that engineering was not for him, that he was too far behind to obtain an engineering degree, that the curriculum would be too much for him to handle, and that he should stick to a major that did not have upper level math and sciences. They asked him if he had taken calculus or trigonometry in high school, because if he had not, he would never make it in engineering.

My son said that every negative thing they told him only fueled him to work harder. Actually, he would laugh at them.

Willie always said, "A person can do whatever they want to do, if they put their mind to it! It may take some a longer time to achieve it than others, but if they don't give up, they will accomplish it, too!"

My son saw a great opportunity to attend classes at Houston Community College. One of the instructors there was an engineer and taught some engineering courses that were required for my son's degree. Willie was able to get a good math and science foundation before transferring to a university, and Houston Community College provided him with local classes with convenient and transferrable hours. While in school, Willie pushed himself like never before. He studied for many hours on the weekends, worked hundreds of math problems, and got so good at calculus that his teacher became suspicious of the high scores that Willie received on his exams. Willie told me that the instructor pulled a desk right beside his and watched him take an exam. I guess the teacher found it hard to believe that a young, hip, black male could score high on calculus exams. Willie excelled in math; he made As in calculus and got a part-time job tutoring mathematics at Houston Community College. He also continued driving trucks locally and took classes at night. After completing all of the necessary classes for his engineering major at the community college, Willie transferred to Prairie View A&M University in the summer of 1998. There, he worked even harder in his engineering classes, and sustained a B average. He graduated from Prairie View in 2000 with honors. He was thirty years old when he finished college, and always told others to never give up on their goals no matter how long it took or how difficult things got. This was a major accomplishment and milestone for my son. When factoring in all that he had been through, no one would have ever predicted that he would graduate with an engineering degree. Willie was very proud of himself, and never doubted that he would succeed.

FOURTH OF JULY WEEKEND

It was the Fourth of July weekend, and Willie had just graduated from college in May. He rented a car to come home for the holidays. His Uncle LC was having a party at his house for his wife and had invited friends and family over. Many of my son's cousins from Rockwood were at the party: Squirk, Q-Baby, Lil' Hoss, and E. Slim; even Cooley's son, Big Luke, was there. My brother had plenty of food and liquor at the party. Throughout the night, people kept going back and forth to the store for ice and other things. Someone used my son's rental car for one of the trips. Later that night, Mike Black had too much to drink and started to get out of control, so Willie decided to leave the party and take Mike Black home. While driving home, Mike Black was still extremely hyped up and would not calm down. Willie drove faster, reaching speeds of up to a hundred miles per hour. As they entered Rockwood, they heard sirens and saw lights from a police car behind them. The officer pulled them over and asked to search the vehicle. Willie agreed because he had nothing to hide. The cop inspected the vehicle, removed a small bag, and immediately called for backup. He placed Willie and Mike Black under arrest for possession of crack cocaine with the intent to distribute. Willie and Mike Black could not believe it! They kept telling the officer that the drugs did not belong to them, and that they did not know how it had gotten there.

The officer knew Willie and Mike Black from Rockwood. Smitty, now a cop, had grown up in the adjacent neighborhood, and they had all played basketball together. Mike Black told Smitty that Willie had graduated from college with an engineering degree, and had gotten out the game a long time ago. They both tried to get through to Smitty that this was a "bunch of bullshit!" Nonetheless, Smitty handcuffed Willie and Mike Black and put them in the police car. The rental car was impounded, and they both spent the night in jail. The incident was an embarrassment. Their names and charges were printed in the local newspaper. All charges were later put on Willie, and he had to get a lawyer to prove his innocence. My son spent the next year driving back and forth between Baton Rouge and Houston for the court proceedings. Fortunately, his attorney got all of the charges dismissed. Willie must not have returned home to visit for maybe two years after that ordeal.

PRIVATE VS. PUBLIC SECTOR

My son was fortunate to get a job right after he graduated. The very next month, he began working the with a highway department for the government in Houston, Texas, as an engineering assistant. His first job assignment was to design and prepare the plans, specifications and estimates for a traffic signal. He also prepared plans for flashing beacons, and signing & striping projects throughout Houston. My son made several safety modifications to intersections and reviewed traffic studies from consultants. He spent five years doing that type of work, and enjoyed it, but decided to leave the highway department for the private sector and earn a higher salary. So, he left his government job to work for a private engineering firm. My son said working for that company was like modern-day slavery. The managers followed their employees to the restrooms. The work hours were horrible; my son said that often he would go in to work at around 7:00 a.m. and not know what time he would be getting out. It could be anywhere from 10:00 p.m. or 11:00 p.m. that night. The company also wanted him to work a lot of weekends and expected him to work those extra hours at his base pay. He was a salaried employee and did not receive overtime pay. My son said that if you were to compare the actual hours that he worked to the salary that they paid him, a fast food restaurant employee probably made more money per hour than he did. Besides, when their projects slowed down, the engineering firm had no problem firing someone. My son went back to work for a government agency after that experience, and said that he would never want to work for a private engineering company again. The only private company he would work for again would be his own. My son realized after that experience that a person had to be in business for himself in order to really get ahead in life. However, if a person was not pursuing a business of his own, he should at least be working to obtain a college degree.

When he returned to the government job, he worked in a roadway design section. My son was eager to learn roadway and bridge design. He spent the next five years designing roads and bridges throughout Houston. Willie was later given the opportunity to lead and manage the roadway and bridge projects. My son enjoyed designing the projects, but he never saw his projects during construction. So, he requested to be transferred to the construction section and get firsthand experience on managing the projects he had once designed.

PROFESSIONAL ENGINEERING LICENSE

Obtaining a professional engineering license was another huge challenge for my son. However, he was determined to obtain it. He had to pass two examinations before becoming a licensed engineer. The first test was the Engineer in Training (EIT) examination: it was an eight-hour exam that covered the fundamentals that all engineering students had learned in their freshmen and sophomore curriculum, and was required in order for an engineer to be considered for the Professional Engineering Exam.

After graduating from college and obtaining four years of engineering experience by working in the industry, the EIT has to submit his Supplemental Experience Record (SER) to an engineering board. The SER is documented work that the EIT has done after graduating from college and entering the engineering field. This experience should be obtained by the EIT while working under the direct supervision of a licensed, professional engineer. Some of the things that an EIT should be doing are designing, constructing, calculating, reviewing, analyzing, and preparing engineering projects in pursuit of becoming a licensed engineer. The board reviews the SER and grants permission for the EIT to take the

Professional Engineering (PE) exam. The PE exam covers junior and senior-level courses, as well as some practical problems that an EIT may experience while on the job. The average EIT has to spend a minimum of three hundred hours preparing for the eight-hour PE exam, which can be a deterrent for most candidates. Willie did not pass either test the first time he took them, but he stayed at it and passed both examinations. In addition, he stayed focused, and with hard work, dedication, and discipline, he obtained his professional engineering license. It was a big deal! He said that it felt almost as good as graduating from college and obtaining his engineering degree. Willie was rewarded with a promotion at his job. His coworkers congratulated him, and his sister, Renae, threw a party at her house and invited friends and family over to celebrate. Even my older sister, Gwen, came, and she hardly ever gets out the house. Everyone had a great time eating, drinking, dancing, and listening to music.

After the party was over and everyone left for home, Willie decided to stop by the old neighborhood, Rockwood, where he had been raised. That was one place he had to visit whenever he came home. I told him that the neighborhood had changed a lot since he'd hung out on the corner, and that it would not be a good idea for him to hang out there anymore.

I told him, "You do not need any more trouble to happen because so much is going on out in those streets, and Willie, you know you don't want to jeopardize your license or career."

My son replied, "I know, Mama, I don't have time for that foolishness anymore."

The next morning, he got out of the bed to eat breakfast. I had prepared grits, turkey bacon, hash browns, and scrambled eggs. It was one of his favorite meals. My son said that as soon as he turned into Rockwood, he saw a familiar face that he had not seen in over a decade. It was Bodacious Bo. He had spent over a decade in prison for his involvement in an armed robbery, and still takes penitentiary chances in the game. He continues to do things and ends up back in prison.

Bodacious Bo was surprised to see my son after so many years. They had attended high school together and had grown up in the same neighborhood.

Bodacious Bo said, "What up, Willie Gat, I heard you were in H-Town."

My son replied, "Yeah, brah, I been out there for a minute. What's been up with you?"

He replied, "Just chillin." Then he told my son, "Damn, Willie Gat, yo' ass have picked up some weight."

My son said, "Yeah, brah, I was hittin' that iron for minute when I was in the military. Alright, Bo, you be cool. I'm about to see what's up in the 'hood, holla at you later, man."

Bodacious Bo said, laughing, "Da 'hood ain't the same, brah!"

My son said that as he continued through Rockwood, he noticed that there was a click house on every street and a lot of abandoned houses.

(I asked him, "What was a click house?" because I am not familiar with all the new terminology they use nowadays.

My son laughed and said, "A dope house, Ma.")

Before he knew it, some guys had yelled out his name. My son said that it was Fuggaboo and Tricky Nick. They had been just little boys when Willie was in the game, and they were happy to see him. Willie said that he pulled his truck over and parked down the street from the click house. He then walked over and started chatting with the boys.

They asked, "What's happenin' like dat and when did you make it down, Willie Gat?"

My son said, "Chillin', I made it down this morning, brah."

Fuggaboo gave Willie a beer, and they continued to kick it about what had been happening in the 'hood. My son said that Fuggaboo and Tricky Nick had grown up to become hardcore gangsters now. Willie noticed that Fuggaboo had a pistol in his back pocket, and while staring at the pistol, he said, "Dang, it's like that now, Fugga?"

Fuggaboo said, "Yeah, mane, thangs done changed out here, brah. Fools will shoot you for just looking at them crazy, you heard me!"

My son said that before he could get halfway through with his beer, two guys pulled up to the click house in an old, brown, beat-up van. The one on the passenger side got out and went inside the click house. A few minutes later, he came out stumbling, blood flowing from his head and down his arm as he fell into the waiting van. Then the driver sped off! My son figured that the drug deal must have gone bad, and that that guy had gotten his wig split. Just as that happened, a crack head walked towards them from down the street, and Fuggaboo asked him, "What's up?"

He wanted to get some drugs, but did not have any money, so Fuggaboo told him to keep it moving. The crack head began to insist that Fuggaboo hook him up because he had been spending money with him all day, and told Fuggaboo that he owed him one.

Then the crack head moved closer to Fuggaboo, rubbing his head and coughing and telling Fuggaboo that he would pay him tomorrow.

The crack head accidentally coughed and spat on Fuggaboo. Angrily, Fuggaboo grabbed his pistol from his back pocket and smacked the crack head in his face. The crack head tried to run off, but was only able to make it about fifty feet down the street before he wobbled, fell into a yard, and passed out.

Then Fuggaboo and Tricky Nick began to argue about some money that Fuggaboo owed Nick. Fuggaboo told him that he did not have it and would pay him later.

Tricky Nick said, "Bitch, you lying. I want my money now, ho!"

Fuggaboo told Tricky Nick, "You betta back up off me, fool!"

Then all of a sudden, Tricky Nick punched Fuggaboo in the jaw and dropped him.

Fuggaboo was dazed for a minute, then got up and pulled his pistol out.

Tricky Nick took off for his car and was about to drive off.

Fuggaboo aimed, but before he could pulled the trigger, Willie yelled out, "Don't do it, Fuggaboo, don't do it!"

That night, Fuggaboo listened to Willie and did not pull the trigger. Fuggaboo told him, "Damn, Willie Gat, you have calm down a lot since back in the day."

My son told Fuggaboo, "Yeah, I have grown up a lot since then, brah."

Then an old female friend who had witnessed the entire incident walked over and said to my son, "So why are you hanging out here now, Willie Gat?"

Willie looked at her and had no answer.

CHAPTER 19

NEW HOUSE
FULFILLMENT

NEW HOUSE

In 2001, my son bought a brand-new, beautiful, brick, single-family home. They had begun constructing it on the fourth of July. It was about 1,600 square feet, and had three bedrooms, two bathrooms, a living room, a two-car garage, a study, and a kitchen with bay windows. My son was going crazy before and during the construction of his house. He could not make up his mind when he was choosing the bricks, paint, tiles, cabinets, and carpet, just to name a few things. He drove by homes to check out the bricks before making a decision. He paid extra to have widows relocated in the house. That son of mine was trying to modify the floor plans, but the builder refused. Willie could not believe that the back of the house did not come with bricks, so he paid extra to have bricks all around the house. He must have stopped by that house every day during construction to check things out. The neighborhood was adjacent to the one in which he lived, which made his visits very easy.

Finally, when my son had made up his mind and knew exactly what he wanted, the builder began to blow him off. Even after he had paid for certain changes to the house, the builder did not adjust to them. Like the additional money Willie had paid for them to not install a window in the back of the house for the living room: my son said that he stopped by one day to check on the progress of the house and saw that the workers had installed the windows.

My son asked the guys why they were installing the window.

The worker responded, "Because that is what the plans show."

My son told the worker not to install the window.

The guy asked my son if this was his house.

My boy replied, "Yes," and the worker did not install the window.

My son went to the builders and asked them why the window was being installed after he had paid extra for it not to be installed.

The builder said that they did not know what happened.

For some strange reason, the builder changed superintendents towards the end of completing my son's home. My son told me that the guy who was in charge, Bobby, got tired of him overseeing everything that he did. He was an easy-going guy and never argued or fussed with Willie, but my son said that he could tell that Bobby was irritated with him, especially whenever Willie went by his field office asking questions and wanting answers for things about the house.

The new guy the builder sent out was named Bubba, and he was a rude and obnoxious person. This man was maybe in his late thirties, muscularly built, six feet, three inches tall, and weighed about 230 pounds. It was October now, and the house was finished. All my son had to do was make the final inspection and get the keys to his brand-new house. During the walk-through, tensions were high, and things had gotten more heated between my son and Bubba.

There were still a few cleanup people in the house doing touchups, and right off my son noticed that the house was kind of chilly.

So he asked Bubba why the house wasn't heating up.

He replied, "The heating unit is probably not working."

So my son said, "Someone needs to get it working."

Bubba replied, "You don't need any heat; it doesn't get that cold in Texas."

My son said that that made his blood boil!

They were doing the walk-through with their shoes off, but my son immediately slapped his tennis shoes on and told Bubba, "Man, that's fucked up! Let's discuss that shit in the backyard. Right now!"

Bubba did not go outside. Instead, he told my son that he did not have to buy the house, walked out the front door, and left.

My son said that he had never felt so many mixed emotions all at one time in his whole life. He went from excitement and joy to anger, hurt, disgust, and disappointment!

Despite all of that work, time, and effort he had put in to get things exactly the way he wanted them, it all seemed to go up in flames at the very end.

My son said that after he cleared his head, he contacted the builder and explained to them what had happened. They sent Bubba back out to the house, and he fixed the problem. It was a brand-new heating unit that only needed a minor adjustment to correct the problem. Fortunately, everything got resolved, and my boy loved his new home—or as he called it, the "bachelor's crib."

Around the time when my son bought his new home, his old buddy from the Army, Gribb, was also out of the military and had purchased a home with his wife, Lena. He and Lena had their first child and were living right outside of Dallas. Gribb had gotten a job working for the United States Postal Service. He and Willie kept in touch and talked on the phone every now and then about their old Army days together. Sadly, an incident occurred to my son's old Army friend. When my son was sick with the flu and on bed rest, he received a disturbing phone call from Lena. She had called to tell my son that Gribb had passed, and could Willie attend the services as a pallbearer?

My son said that he was blown away by the news!

He asked Lena, "What happen?"

Lena told my son that one afternoon, Gribb had had a really bad headache and insisted that she take him to the hospital. She said that on the way there, Gribb's head was swelling, but she managed to get him to a doctor.

Unfortunately, Gribb did not make it, and died that day at the hospital. He was only thirty years old.

My son told Lena, "Dang Lena, I am sorry for your loss, and I hate to hear that about my boy. But I am in bed sick as a dog with the flu and cannot make it to the funeral."

My son told Lena to stay strong for Lil' Gribb, and wished them well. He also told Lena to call him if they ever needed something, and to keep in touch.

HOUSTON VISITS

We loved to visit my son in Houston. We would usually go during the summer and football season. We all would load up, sometimes eight or ten people, and hit the road when Southern University was either playing Prairie View A&M University or Texas Southern University. Most of us were Southern University graduates and loved to go to their games. My son enjoyed the games, too. He had love for Southern and Prairie View. Willie had attended Southern University back in 1989, and was a Prairie View A&M graduate. So when the two schools played one another, he just wanted to see a good game.

My son had become an excellent cook over the years, and he loved outdoor cooking. Grilling steaks, barbecuing, boiling seafood, and frying turkeys were some of his favorite ways to cook. When crawfish season was in, my son would get up early in the morning to buy the crawfish. Then he would go by the grocery store and get all the ingredients for the crawfish boil. He would pick up Louisiana Crawfish Boil, hot sauce, yellow onion, lemon juice, butter, beef sausages, red potatoes, and corn. He would place the crawfish in the cooler under bags of ice. The crawfish would then hibernate until he was ready to boil them later that day. My son was a perfectionist about everything he did. Whatever he was doing had to be planned and just right. Before he boiled the crawfish, Willie would purge them so that they would not have a muddy taste to them. He would place the live crawfish in a cooler and sprinkle salt over them. He would then hose the crawfish with running water until the water exiting the cooler was clear. Next, he would get his burner out, connect it to the propane tank, and light it. Then he added water in the stainless steel boiling pot and set it on the burner.

I remember asking him, "How do you know the amount of water to add in the pot?"

He responded, "I know from boiling them all the time, Ma, and I know how much water to add for a basket full of crawfish. However, if someone did not know how much water to add for their crawfish, what they would need to do is place the basket with the crawfish into the pot and add water until it covered the seafood, then remove the basket with the crawfish, and the remaining water in the pot is what they would need for their boil."

My son would then begin to get his boil ready. He would cut one whole yellow onion, add the Louisiana Crawfish Boil, lemon juice, butter, and hot sauce, and stir everything with this gigantic plastic spoon. I have never seen a plastic spoon that big, and asked him where he'd gotten it. My son said that he'd bought it at the flea market, but had never seen one like that again.

After the fire got going, it did not take long before the water and ingredients came to a rolling boil. My son dropped his basket full of crawfish into the boil. He let the crawfish boil for about five minutes, and I could see the bright red crawfish rise to the top of the pot. My son took the crawfish out and placed them in a cooler. He had about three different coolers out there for mild, spicy, and "Butta Saucy" crawfish. He loved to use this butter sauce recipe that he'd gotten from his cousin on his daddy's side of the family in New Orleans. It tastes really good on seafood. He used melted butter, hot sauce, garlic powder, and other special seasonings. My son changed the sauce up a little bit and put it over the crawfish in the cooler after he did his so-called "cooler trick."

His "cooler trick" consisted of sprinkling extra Louisiana Crawfish Boil over the hot, steaming crawfish and shaking the cooler several times. That steam and seasoning just seemed to penetrate the crawfish, and made them very tasty! The more seasoning he added, the spicier the crawfish would be. He boiled the beef sausages, potatoes, and corn last.

If my son was not boiling crawfish when we came to visit, he was grilling. My boy had several charcoal grills and smokers, but he felt that the best way to grill a steak was with a gas grill. He loved to grill rib eye steaks. He bought a gas grill just to cook the steaks. My son also liked to grill chicken, fajitas, hamburgers, and sausages with his charcoal grill. He has one grill specifically for just smoking food. He loved to marinate the steaks with Worcestershire sauce for a few hours in the refrigerator, then let them sit out at room temperature before grilling them. He would always say, "Never place a cold steak on the grizzle." Before he placed the steaks on the grill, he rubbed them with black pepper and sprinkled a little salt on them.

Willie rubbed a lot of steak seasoning into the steaks, but he does not put in as much as he used to because it is loaded with sodium. My son has been trying to eat healthier now, even cutting back on fried and fast foods and eating more baked chicken and fish, and encourages us to do the same. However, he grills the steaks to our preference. I like my steak well done, but my son likes his medium well.

After he took the steaks off the grill, Willie would place a scoop of butter on them. We would eat a fresh salad and baked potato with the steaks.

I would say, "Yummy and delicious, I'm talking about good eating!"

If my son is not grilling, he is cooking fish. He loves to bake tilapia and prepare blackened catfish. That baked tilapia is so good and tasty. My son loves to coat the tilapia with extra virgin olive oil. He then sprinkles black pepper and Cajun seasoning on it. Before placing it in the oven, my son puts butter and pours a little lemon juice on it. He covers the pan with aluminum foil and bakes it at 375 degrees for twenty-five minutes. After that, he lets it broil for two to three minutes. Cooking fish like this is healthy and makes it taste very good.

The blackened catfish is very good, too. My son also coats the catfish with extra virgin olive oil. He sprinkles Cajun seasoning on it and adds lots of black pepper to it. My son cooks the seasoned catfish in butter with a flat, black, cast-iron skillet. He turns it until the catfish is blackened and serves it with sautéed shrimp. The sautéed shrimp is pretty much cooked the same way as the blackened catfish, but sometimes he adds sliced onions while he is cooking it.

Before we all get ready to head back to Louisiana, you know we have to eat a big breakfast. I would get up early that morning to cook grits, eggs, and bacon. However, my son insists on cooking the hash browns. He makes them really good, too; they taste just like some of the restaurants' hash browns. The first thing he does is place the shoestring hash browns in a bowl of water for them to thaw out. Then he cooks them in butter with the flat, black, cast-iron skillet. He sprinkles a little salt and pepper over them as they cook.

My son loves say, "Nobody touches the hash browns!" He lets them cook without flipping or stirring them. They can get really crispy, if you prefer them that way.

After that delicious breakfast, we are set for our four-and-a-half-hour drive home to Louisiana.

CHAPTER 20

WHERE ARE THEY NOW
FINAL WORDS

CHOICES

My son often returns home to visit for holidays and other family events. Honestly, I get really nervous every time he comes home to visit because he loves to hang out in the streets and visit Rockwood to see his family and homeboys. He tells me about how all of his boys are gone. They're either dead, in jail, or hooked on drugs. My son wonders if he would have finished college if he never got out the game, or if he would have ended up dead or in prison!

Even the other two gang members who confronted him on the night of the shooting are off the streets. One was allegedly shot and killed a few years after the confrontation with my son. The word on the street is that the other one is in prison for the attempted murder of an undercover police officer. He allegedly shot a narcotics agent seven times during a drug deal, and I think he received seventy-two years in prison for his crime.

My son calls home all the time to see how the family is doing. He especially asks about his little brother, Gerrod, who looks up to him. I always tell my son the truth about what is going on at home. The lifestyle that he lived negatively influenced his little brother and cousins. They all wanted to be in the game and have picked up where he left off.

Once, I told him, "Gerrod runs the streets like you use too. They all saw the trouble you were in and still chose to go down that road. Hopefully, when you come home to visit, you can talk to them."

My son said, "I will talk to them, but we both know these things should be addressed at a very early age." My son also said, "I am not going to preach to them, because nobody could tell me anything when I was in the game."

He really feels that the best thing he can do now is to lead by example.

One day, my daughter, Renae, and I were at the hair salon when I noticed a man staring at us. For some reason, he would not stop staring, and then he walked over to us and called us by our names.

However, we still did not know who this man was, and he said, "I cannot believe you all do not know who I am. It's me, Mo' Money!"

We were both blown away; we jumped up and gave him a big hug and asked him how he was doing.

He replied, "I'm good. I came by the salon to see a friend."

He asked me how Willie Gat was doing.

I told him that Willie was doing fine, and Mo' Money gave me his number so my son could give him a call.

I called my son and told him that Renae and I had run into Mo' Money and had not recognized him. He had gotten really big and muscular with tattoos all over him. He was no longer the slender Mo' Money we had known.

My son called Mo' Money and spoke with him, and they laughed and talked about old times. Also, my son asked Mo' Money if he were still in the game.

Mo' Money told my son, "I'm in it to the end!"

My son knew that Mo' Money had been in the game for a long time now, and figured that he would have not responded any differently.

Mike Black and my son talk on the phone often and see one another when Willie is home visiting. Things have not changed much for Willie's cousin, though; he has spent some time in prison for robbery and other burglary offenses. He is still using cocaine and doing his thing in the streets.

However, Mike Black did tell my son, "Damn, man, I gotta get this gorilla off my fuckin' back!"

My son badly wants to help his cousin beat that dreadful habit, but knows that Mike Black is the only one who can truly end the addiction.

The children's father, Dumplin, passed away on June 1, 2008 from complications of a brain aneurism. He was only fifty-five years old.

Through all of his hard work and perseverance, my son finished college and obtained a professional engineering license. He also achieved one of his long-term goals and owns his own engineering company. I am very proud of my son's success, and very happy that he got out the game.

CONCLUSION

Raising kids as a single parent is really difficult. My son put a few gray strings in my hair that I did not expect this soon. Our sons do not realize how much heartache and pain they put their poor mothers through when they participate in foolishness. Trouble is so easy to get into, and very hard to get out of. My son got lucky—things could have turned out drastically different for him. He could have been killed or thrown in jail for the rest of his life, or even stuck in the game. I am fortunate that things worked out for him. I hope that by reading this book, anyone who may have encountered a similar situation can make use of our experiences.

ACKNOWLEDGEMENTS

First of all, my son and I would like to thank family and friends for allowing us the opportunity to include them in this book. We would also like to thank the people who read the material and offered their opinions and advice. To Linda, Renee, Olga, Burt, and "Big Unc"—special thanks for devoting your time to read the rough drafts and for encouraging me to write more.